Monstrosity, Humanity

MM Schreier

Published by MM Schreier, 2024.

MONSTROSITY, HUMANITY

First edition. March 29, 2024.

ISBN: 979-8224864874

Written by MM Schreier.

Table of Contents

for all those dude bros who told me "girls" can't write horror

and to those who told me to do it anyway

This book is a horror collection and contains mature themes that may not be suitable for all readers.

While fear, monsters, ghosts, murder, and mayhem are to be expected, additional sensitive subjects including child death and domestic violence are touched upon.

It Tastes of Salt and Terror

The small creature's scream cuts off with a gurgle. Long ears fall limp. The sudden silence ricochets through my head. Deafening. White fur turns red. Coppery rivulets trickle down my chin as I gobble the steaming entrails. I crack bones and suck out the marrow. It does nothing to ease the gnawing in my belly.

Hunger drives me onward.

The promise of frost scents the air; I throw back my head and howl. Short days loom ahead—cold, lean times.

I need to feed. To rend flesh, to consume, to gorge.

No matter how I try, the void cannot be filled.

#

Seamus eyed the dried leaves on the floor of the Adirondack Great Camp. He added "replace windows" to his mental to-do list. Another renovation to an abandoned historical site that had once catered to Vanderbilts and Rockefellers.

Breathing deep, he savored the nostalgic remnants of a gilded age. And dust. Lots of dust. He wrinkled his nose and surveyed the room. A fieldstone fireplace dominated the back wall while exposed beams crossed overhead, draped in shawls of spider silk. Wide-board pine lay underfoot, waiting to be restored to honeyed glory. So much potential.

Seamus grinned as his phone played a little boom chick-a bowwow tone. "Darling."

Carson didn't bother with hello. "So? How does it look?"

"It looks like money." For a moment, Seamus reveled in a luxurious fantasy. Crisp, white tablecloths, sparkling crystal, and two-hundred-dollars-a-plate delicacies.

"It had better. You're sinking the profits from all three of our restaurants into this."

"We'll make it back. And then some. I promise." Seamus clucked his tongue; Carson never saw the big picture. "The front door needs replacing, but the place is mostly in good shape. We add in a commercial kitchen and some amenities for the guest rooms—"

Carson snorted. "What kind of 'amenities' and what'll they cost me?"

"Gas inserts for the fireplaces, for starters. Cozy. And keeps the city slickers from burning the place down trying to light a fire."

"Remind me again why the 'city slickers' are going to pay lots of money to stay in a nineteenth century lodge in the middle of nowhere?"

Seamus clenched his jaw and counted to five in his head before answering the question. Again. "Because, sweetheart, when I'm through with it, this is going to be the most romantic, upscale, lakeside destination getaway in the Northeast. And it won't just be 'lots of money.' It will be obscene amounts of cash."

Gravel crunched in the driveway, and Seamus glanced out the window. "Gotta go. The contractor's here. We'll talk later."

#

She's crying again. How can there be tears when she's dead and gone? She cradles her swollen belly and begs me not to go. One last hunt before the snows come, I tell her. So easy to dismiss her concerns. The furs bring good money. She enjoys the lifestyle, does she not?

Her hair's like sunshine. But her face is fluid—moonlight on water. Black blood streams between her thighs. The child kills her, but I'm not there to see. By the time the news comes, the hunger already has me in its grip.

I shake my head as the fractured Then blends with Now.

Then, I hunted for pelts. For the wealth. Now, I simply feed.

I eat and eat, and still I starve.

Once again, I stalk the fur-beasts. I cannot remember their names. It matters not, as one by one I hunt them down. The cunning silver-grey shadows who deal death in packs. The great, clawed fish-eater that slumbers through the long-night season. The rare, tawny shadow, all muscle and liquid elegance. It puts up a fight. Hissing. Lips peel back over wicked fangs.

I consume them all. And still I hunger. They are not enough.

The forbidden flesh calls to me. Perhaps its taboo sweetness will satiate.

I come down off the mountain.

#

The setting sun painted streaks of rose and lilac across the lake. Seamus pulled into the lodge's parking lot and frowned as the construction foreman tossed his toolbox into the back of a rusty pickup. It was the only other vehicle in the lot.

"Hey, Morris! Where is everyone?"

The contractor glanced at the skyline. "Done for the day."

"Done? It's not even six o'clock."

A shadow crossed the foreman's face. "Locals won't work past sunset."

Seamus huffed. "Are you kidding me? Winter's around the corner, and I need this place buttoned up before the snow flies!"

"We're on schedule. The Halon fire suppression system is installed. Appliances arrive next week. The plumber turned the water on this morning." Morris ran a hand through his hair, his eyes shifting away from the sheet of plastic covering the doorway.

"Great. Aside from the giant freaking hole in the front of the building." Seamus glowered. "And what do you mean, no one works after dark?"

"Bad things happen 'round here. Hikers disappear. Campsites ravaged, the people never found." Morris took a shaky breath. "The other day, a couple found a dead mountain lion up on the pass."

Seamus raised an eyebrow.

"Something ripped it apart. Left a trail of blood 'cross a mile of trail." Morris swallowed. "Whatever can do that, I sure as hell don't want to meet it." Without another word, he hopped in his truck and drove off.

The hairs on the back of Seamus's neck stood on end. He'd overheard the workmen whispering; a rumor that something sinister stalked the High Peaks—an uncanny creature they'd been reluctant to name.

He drummed his fingers on the hood of his Lexus. Mountain lions were elusive. It would take a cunning hunter to track and kill one.

Seamus shrugged, putting a more realistic spin on the rumors. The couple had probably stumbled upon the remains of a rabbit, left by a coyote, and got excited over nothing. The missing hikers? It was the damned wilderness. Easy to get lost.

Rolling his eyes, he pushed aside the plastic sheeting covering the lodge's gaping doorway. He was curious to see how the renovations were coming along.

#

Once again, Then fills my head.

The sun casts bloody shadows on the frozen lake. A warning. I shouldn't be here. She told me not to come. I should've listened.

Snowdrifts block the lodge's door, the aftermath of an unexpected nor'easter. My fellow hunter feeds furniture to the fire until there's nothing left to burn. The flames die. Hoarfrost turns my beard white, making me old before my time.

Our provisions run dry, and a pang stabs my middle. The stabbing becomes agony; a sharp-toothed creature burrowing through my insides. It spreads until the hunger fills me, leaving no room for anything else.

My companion no longer moves. He stares at me with fixed, unseeing eyes. Ravenous and dizzy, my vision blurs.

Madness descends.

When I wake, I am alone. Alone with a ravaged corpse and an insatiable craving for more flesh. My hands are sticky, stained dark. I lick them clean.

I claw at my face and the snow fades away. It is not the long-night season. No, not yet.

The images of Then scatter like bloated, wriggling vermin from beneath an overturned log. Their countless feet tickle my brain. Little thoughts that meant something once.

If I squash them, will they stop tormenting me?

In the Now, a void fills me. I can taste the echo of blood on my tongue. My stomach growls.

I skulk closer to the old lodge, drawn by the scent of men, driven by my need to feed.

#

Seamus hummed to himself as he caressed the new stainless steel prep tables in the kitchen. Muscle-memory from his years as a sous chef made his fingers itch to dice and julienne. Simpler days, when he cooked instead of managed. Sighing, he dismissed the memory. If he hadn't worked his ass off, scraped together all his savings and bought that first restaurant, he'd have never met Carson.

With a mischievous smile, Seamus fished his cell from his pocket, intending to send his partner a steamy text. Carson would be at one of their restaurants at this hour, running around like a dervish, poking into everyone's business. The text would get him flustered. Adorable. He'd blush, then grumble at any of the staff who caught him red-faced. Seamus chuckled and tapped out a few words. The screen chirruped once and went black.

"Dammit." He'd left his charger at the motel. His mood soured.

He sniffed and something putrid filled his nostrils, like a dead rat in the wall. No, more like a dozen dead rats in the wall. He gagged and covered his nose with his sleeve. The odor drifted from the foyer and he crossed the room to investigate. The stench of rot intensified, and his eyes watered.

Outside, the last rays of a dying sun streamed through the trees, backlighting the sheet in the doorway. A too-tall, man-shaped shadow stood on the other side.

"Hello?" Seamus's voice quivered. "Can I help you?"

The silhouette had hunched shoulders and sticklike arms and legs. Plastic fluttered, as if a deep breath sucked the air out. The shadow keened, the drawn out, high-pitched wail slowly rising in a desperate urgency.

With sweaty palms, Seamus reached down to pick up a hammer the workmen had left behind. "This is private property—"

Curved claws shredded the plastic, and an emaciated giant burst into the room.

The beast towered over Seamus, head brushing the beams. It was as if a man had been stretched to a great height, then starved. Every joint protruded from lanky limbs, the muscles wasted. Rotting, ash-grey skin sloughed off its ribcage, showing flashes of white bone underneath. The shrunken flesh on its face pulled tight, giving it a skull-like appearance. Rusty red dripped from its teeth. It had chewed off its own lips with jagged, broken teeth.

Seamus opened his mouth, but his tongue felt wooden, stoppering a scream in his throat. The hammer clattered to the floor, numb fingers unable to maintain his grip. The demon's eyes glowed catlike in the shadows, yet were all too human, the whites bloodshot and tinged yellow. They glittered feverishly, filled with madness and hunger.

#

Bitter sweat fills the air and drool oozes over my chin. I can almost taste the sweetness of his flesh. My teeth gnash on their own, as if they already bite and chew.

Run, little tidbit. It's more fun if I chase you. Fear flavors the meat.

He doesn't move. I can smell his horror. It paralyzes him.

Swifter than the wind, I'm on him, slamming him into the wall. I lean down and lick his smooth cheek. It tastes of salt and terror. A hint of greed.

Mine or his?

He whimpers.

The hunger makes demands of me. Bite. Tear. Gorge.

But no. I won't let it own me. Not yet. Before long, the darkness will crash down. For now, I want to toy with my food.

Perhaps, just a quick nibble, before I give him another chance to flee. Rip off one of the fleshy bits from the side of his head.

Before I can decide, he finds his courage. Ducking under my arm, he bolts.

The hunt is on.

#

Feet pounding, Seamus darted through the shredded plastic and into the night. The sun had slipped behind the mountains and twisted shadows stretched across the parking lot, reaching out as if alive. The shiny Lexus beckoned, an oasis in the desert of gravel.

Seamus turned out his pockets, grasping for his keys. Empty. Had he set them down in the kitchen? He recalled the jangle of metal on metal as he'd tossed them on the prep table.

Behind him, the tattered plastic sheet crackled.

On gangly limbs, the creature closed half the distance before Seamus registered it was coming. Despite its atrophied form, it moved with the speed of a wolf and the boneless grace of a wildcat. Its bloody mouth stretched in a lipless grin.

Seamus sprinted towards the cover of the woods. The wilderness swallowed him, thorns tearing at his clothes. Gnarled tree limbs reached down to claw at his hair, as if the forest sensed an intruder.

#

Tsk tsk. This is my domain.

I follow my prey, jumping from shadow to shadow. They welcome me in their cold embrace, recognizing me as kin.

His hair is the same sunshiny hue as hers.

The hunger bids me to hurry. To end it swiftly. Only then can I fill my belly. Devour his flesh. Surely it will ease this ever-present, hollow ache.

She disapproves.

I falter.

Two bright lights twinkle in the sky. Her eyes, looking down on me from the heavens. The block of ice behind my breastbone cracks.

Ahead, I catch a flash of yellow between the trees. Black spots fill my vision. A mewling whine bubbles from my throat as need slices through me.

She belongs Then. This is Now. Her memory cannot save me from the hunger.

The wind picks up, sweeping dark clouds across the sky. The stars wink out.

I resume the hunt and let the darkness take me.

#

Brambles snagged Seamus's sweater as he staggered through the forest. Blood trickled where a branch had whipped across his face. The landscape sloped upward, and his thighs burned. He leaned against a tree trunk, sucking down the crisp night air. Breath rattled in his chest.

From lower down the mountain, the beast bayed. A forlorn yearning that sent goosebumps rippling down Seamus's arms. He pushed off the tree and stumbled onward.

Ahead, a ghostly light beckoned. The ground grew rocky as the trees thinned. Icy fingers of wind snaked down his collar. They brought with them the fetid stench of rotting flesh.

The demon closed.

Seamus forced his feet to move faster. He held to the irrational thought that if he could just get to the light, he'd be safe. A stone turned underfoot, and he pitched forward. Trousers torn, he crawled out of the woods on bloody knees. The clearing opened onto a rock shelf. Beyond the edge, a ravine promised a long fall.

Overhead, the moon cast a bright ribbon through a break in the clouds. In the silver light, a snowflake drifted, caught in a slow-motion downward spiral. It landed on his cheek, biting like a tiny frozen serpent.

Carson loved the first snowfall of the season. Seamus sobbed his partner's name, uncertain if it was a cry for help or forgiveness.

In the tree line, darkness bulged. The demon disentangled itself from the shadows and howled at the moon. Seamus scrabbled back, fingernails splintering on the rock, until he teetered on the edge of the cliff. Before he could fall, claws clamped around his ankle, grinding the bones together.

The creature dragged him close, its sticklike limbs filled with uncanny strength.

#

When I wake, I am once again alone with a despoiled corpse.

The flesh is stripped. The bones are cracked and gnawed on. There is hair in my teeth and the taste of gristle on my tongue.

I should be sated, stomach bloated with my gluttony.

But no. My shadow casts long and thin on the blood-soaked ground.

I have fed and grown, though. My bones feel stretched.

Snow falls, but I don't suffer the cold.

There's only hunger.

No matter how I try, the void cannot be filled.

Ghost Rain

The trains don't run anymore, yet I still find myself out here on this abandoned stretch of railway, waiting for a midnight express that never arrives. I have nowhere better to go.

Once, the big diesel engines roared up and down the parallel tracks, moving raw coal and livestock. Years passed, and they added passenger cars. I'd find myself haunting the culvert with a half-wild gang of colt-limbed ragamuffins. The trains would whoosh by, blowing back our hair.

Some of the band would throw stones at the speeding cars, but I'd just wave, staring green-eyed at the fancy city folk headed to the Berkshires to spend the summer holidays in their vacation homes. I'd try to picture myself on the other side of the train windows, dressed in an over-starched jacket and silken gloves, peering down my nose at the rock-throwing urchins. The luxury was hard to imagine.

Soot-gray clouds hide the stars, and it's been some time since anyone bothered to send power to the nearby tenements. The darkness doesn't bother me. My feet know the way better than my eyes. I flip up my collar against the echo of rain, dampness I sense rather than feel.

When I reach the tracks, I climb the verge to walk between the parallel lines. I'm surprised the grass hasn't grown tall between the ties. It's as if the trains stopped yesterday, not decades ago. I listen for the gang, shrieking in a paradox-twist of terror and delight. If we timed it right and remained statue-still as the Northbound and Southbound trains passed by on either side, it felt like being in the eye of a tornado.

The frozen-time feeling is a misguided fantasy. Tonight, there's no shrill whistle, no clatter of wheels on tracks. No pack of untamed boys, trading insults and laughter. There's only silence. And the damned not-rain.

I turn towards the horizon, a jigsaw of broken-toothed mountains. Somewhere above, there's a copper coin moon behind the clouds. It leaks an eerie, russet halo over the distant peaks. The light doesn't illuminate the tracks, but simply paints bloodshot shadows across the darker charcoal and sable of the night.

My traitorous feet begin to walk. They must know where we are going, even if I don't. The dream-like trance somehow reminds me I'm supposed to count the electric poles that follow alongside the tracks. I'm not sure why, but I do it anyway.

One.

Four.

Eleven.

Seventeen.

Here.

I glance around, uncertain where *here* is. It looks just like all the rest, an endless expanse of unbroken steel rails, crossed by wooden ties. Though I know I've been walking for a while—hours, days, years—I seem no closer to the mountains. A prickle runs through me, the feeling of a horde of invisible insects swarming over my skin.

My legs jerk, and like a marionette controlled by an unseen hand, I take a lurching step forward, then sink to my knees. Everything feels strangely familiar—both forgotten, and on the tip of my tongue.

The not-quite-rain comes down harder. I can see it sheeting over the trees and splashing off the rails, but my face remains dry. With trembling fingers, I reach for the rail. The wet metal thrums. There's a train coming.

That's a waste of a good penny.

The bodiless voice shocks me, but I still have no control over my limbs. There's only the phantom coin in my hand. It's harder to position than I thought it would be. The rain-slick rail vibrates, announcing the oncoming midnight express and the damned penny keeps sliding off.

A whistle screams—the echo of a memory, both piercing and muffled.

Come on, Trevor!

Move it!

Get away from there!

Huffing, I ignore the spectral appeals of my friends and reposition the penny. If that fancy git at the station can flatten one, so can I. He had flourished the squashed bit of metal, his chest puffed in his expensive coat. One eyebrow cocked, as if to say he was better than me. Smarter, braver. I had wanted to knock the smug look off his face with my fist; show him his money didn't make it true.

I can hardly remember what he looked like anymore. For a moment, my hand hovers over the rail. I could give up. Pocket the penny and go to Woolworth's in the morning to buy a chewy, chocolaty Tootsie Roll instead. My mouth waters; I can almost taste it.

No. Woolworth's closed a long time ago.

Water drips off my nose, and though I try to dash it away, there's no texture to the not-rain. The penny jumps again, but I catch it before it gets lost in the gravel between ties. Maybe if I put it closer to the base plate, there'll be less vibration? Or I could just hold it in place and jump back at the last minute. I'm definitely wilier than that braggart rich kid, flashing his paper-thin oval of copper.

I can do this. I already did this? Once again, the invisible bugs dance across my neck.

A light flares, white and bright as the train barrels closer.

Trevor!

The squeal of metal on metal drowns out the shout, and the train's headlight consumes me. Inside fractured eternity, I fly.

I fly, and I remember.

How many times now has the train sent me sprawling, broken and bleeding?

It takes only heartbeats to go from tumbling through the air to landing flat on my back. The rumble of the train fades. I try to shake my head, but the puppet master is still in control of my limbs. It's fine. If I were in control, there'd only be a pain I don't want to remember.

The strings force me to look, eyes wide. Inky spiderwebs crowd the edges of my vision, but the bloody moonlight reflects off the flattened coin on the rail, forcing me to see my own hubris. I blink the ghostly rain out of my eyes, pretend I can feel the cold water dripping down my collar. Somewhere in the distance, I can almost hear voices crying. Then the dark webs blot out the light.

Blink.

The trains don't run anymore, yet I still find myself out here on this abandoned stretch of railway, waiting for a midnight express that never arrives. I have nowhere better to go.

Lemon Scented Bleach

Maribell cut a peanut butter sandwich on the diagonal and arranged the halves on a plate like a butterfly. Humming to herself, she set lunch on the table and cleared away the untouched breakfast dishes. Her lips twisted in a rueful grin as she took the bowl over to the double stainless-steel sink—Basil hated oatmeal, simply refused to eat it. After scraping out the congealed mess, she opened the tap and flipped on the disposal.

Unseen blades hummed, and she wondered what it would sound like if she stuck her hand in. Would it crunch, like the time she'd accidentally dropped in a chicken bone? She shrugged and turned the disposal and the water off, then set the bowl in the other side of the sink. The dishes could wait until later.

Maribell had one foot on the stairs when a buzzer stopped her. She turned and headed into the laundry room. Opening the dryer, she breathed in the clean, lavender scent. It was the closest she got to a spa treatment these days. Dryer sheets as aromatherapy. She snorted. Grabbing an armful of clothes, she hugged them to her chest before dumping the pile on the top of the washer to fold.

Laundry was a never-ending battle for a mom of a toddler. Countless, adorable pairs of tiny shorts. A dozen little socks with no matches. A small t-shirt with a reddish blotch on it. Cherry Kool-aid? Maribell frowned as she dabbed spot remover on the splotch. She threw it into the washer for another round and hoped the stain hadn't set. It was Basil's favorite shirt, the one with a funny yellow cartoon character on it. She remembered him wearing it on their annual summer trip to the beach. It had been a perfect day filled with ice cream cones and sandcastles and the squeals of laughter when foamy waves crashed over their toes.

Maribell wished she could recapture that feeling back when they'd been so blissful. Before the knock came at the door. Before her backside went numb sitting on a flimsy folding chair, dressed in all black. Before two strangers, in crisp blue coats and shiny brass buttons, handed her a folded flag while Taps played in the background. As if all that bullshit, stoic Marine Corps ceremony could help her explain to a three-year-old why Daddy wasn't coming home. She sagged into the pile of laundry and let the still warm fabric muffle her sobs.

When the tears played out, Maribell sniffed and, unthinking, rubbed her eyes with the closest thing at hand. A dark smudge came away on the white ribs of a mateless sock.

"Dang it!"

She sighed and grabbed the spot remover again. Wearing mascara was pointless. It was a race each day to see what would set her off. The tears inevitably spoiled her careful applique. But makeup was a habit, and all the righteous grief pamphlets and nosey advice givers advocated for sticking to a routine. Besides, there was Basil to think about. He didn't need to see a washed out, lifeless, zombie of a mom.

She scrubbed at the black mark. It didn't budge. A bubble of laughter tickled her throat. How could a few tears melt waterproof mascara, but the extra strength stain remover was useless? Maribell squashed down the laughter, ignoring its maniacal edge, and grabbed the bleach.

The bottle was a cheery white and yellow with bold letters splashed across the label. *Fresh new scent* and *Made with real lemons!* Maribell clucked her tongue.

"What a world. The bleach is made with real lemons, and my iced tea is artificially flavored."

She twisted off the cap and inhaled. Chlorine and lemon fought for dominance and the scent made her lightheaded. What would it taste like? Perhaps it would burn going down, like the whiskey she hid on top of the fridge. Lemony fire. The plastic bleach bottle trembled in her hand and her thoughts buzzed. Eyes watering, she shook her head.

Buzz. Buzz. Buzz.

"Coming!"

Maribell thunked the bottle down, bleach slopping over her fingers, and dashed to the kitchen. She arrived just in time to see the pre-school's number flash across her phone display before the screen went dark. Heat prickled her skin as the chemicals began to burn. She ran water over her hand and waited for her phone to ding with a new voicemail. It never did.

Perhaps after a half-dozen messages, the teacher had finally realized she wasn't going to return his calls. She didn't have the energy. Didn't they understand she couldn't send Basil back to school? It was just too much right now.

The water soothed her reddened skin, cool against the bleach burn. Maribell glanced down. Dishes were piling up—it was her least favorite chore. It was easy to leave crusty bowls in the sink, fill them with water, and tell herself they needed to soak.

A jelly-gummed knife caught her eye, and her stomach roiled. Basil hated jelly, especially strawberry. How could she mess that up? She grabbed a dish towel and patted her hands dry before spinning around to double check the sandwich on the table. She sagged and flopped down in the chair. Just peanut butter. Tears pricked her eyes, and she blinked them back. Stupid.

No, not stupid. Exhausted. She barely slept. The bottle of untouched sleeping pills mocked her each night when she brushed her teeth, but she refused to take them. They made her feel fuzzy. She was a single mom now; she needed to stay alert. For Basil. Everything was for Basil.

Maribell gathered herself and stood. She turned her back on the sink and the butterflied sandwich and crossed into the living room. In contrast to the growing pile of dirty dishes, the large common room was tidy. Almost too clean. She looked around for something to straighten. With a vigorous whack, she fluffed the already plump throw pillows and re-stacked the coasters on the coffee table. She glowered at the bookshelves, the titles neatly arranged, side-by-side. A finger trailed across the lowboy came away dust-free.

Something neon yellow peeped out from under the couch.

"A-ha!" Maribell pounced and fished out a toy truck. "You belong upstairs."

Triumphant, she marched towards the front hall. At the foot of the stairs, she hesitated. A fat, brown spider lounged on the bottom step. She considered squashing it. No. She taught Basil to have compassion for living things. Spiders and ants got relocated outside. Flies were swished out open windows.

Maribell waffled. Basil would never know. A quick stomp and a swipe of a paper towel, and there'd be no evidence left behind. No. She'd trained herself not to swear, even when little ears weren't listening. She could do the same here.

With a suppressed shudder, Maribell grabbed an unopened bill off the end table and coaxed the hairy monstrosity onto the envelope. She studiously ignored the big red letters shouting *final notice.* They wouldn't dare turn the lights out on a war hero's widow and child.

Taking care not to drop the spider—or let it scuttle up her arm—she carried it to the back door. She twisted the knob, whipped open the door, and shook the intruder out into the yard. As she did, something leaning against the side of the house shifted and fell against the step with the clank of metal against concrete.

Maribell jumped back, startled. Her good garden spade, caked with dirt, lay sprawled on the ground.

"Basil!" She stomped back through the living room, into the front hall, and headed up the stairs. "How many times do I have to tell you—Mommy's garden tools aren't toys!" She strode down the hall. "Basil?"

Maribell pushed open the door to her son's room. It was dark and stifling with the drapes drawn and windows closed.

"Come on, buddy. It's time for lunch."

The lemony scent of bleach burned her nose. "Basil?"

Despite the stuffiness, a shiver ran up her spine, as if the spider was back, feather touch footsteps crawling across her skin. She threw back the curtains to let golden sunshine flood through the window. The light pooled across the floor, illuminating a discolored spot on the carpet. The room was empty. Shiver forgotten, sweat trickled down her back.

Something dark fluttered at the edge of her memory. She pushed it away.

"Basil! Where are you?"

Urgency pressed her feet in motion, and she flew down the hall. The dark thing pursued her, whispering horrors in her ears.

Lies.

Frantic, Maribell checked all of Basil's favorite hiding places. Under her big four-poster bed, in the hall closet, behind the sofa. He wasn't there. He wasn't anywhere. Her heart raced as bile clawed its way up to scorch the back of her throat.

Feeding on her terror, the shadow-memory grew. It loomed over her like some dark specter and forced fractured, bleach-coated images into her mind's eye. They stabbed like shards of glass.

A stained t-shirt.

The muddy spade.

A poorly cleaned carpet.

She grabbed her head and moaned, "No, no, no..."

The dark thing laughed. *Yes.* It showed her a knife in her hands. Not smeared with strawberry jelly, but dripping blood. The knife had clattered as she had dropped it in the kitchen sink. She'd felt nothing, filled by an icy void.

Maribell staggered into the master bathroom, legs leaden. Her head pounded and her ears rang with the silent echoes of a child's screams. In the mirror, a stranger with hollow cheeks stared back at her. Smudges of mascara ran beneath flat, expressionless eyes. Gray. Like Basil's.

On the edge of the sink, an orange plastic bottle called to her with a siren song of oblivion.

She turned her back on the memory monster and shot a stern look at her reflection.

"We should put those away. Basil could get into them."

Don't worry. He knows he's not allowed in our bathroom.

"When do little boys listen?"

Well, then. Get rid of them.

Maribell's reflection nodded in approval as trembling fingers reached for the pill bottle. It took several tries to open the childproof cap. Yellow ovals spilled into her palm and she swallowed them dry.

Good, good. All of them now. It's dangerous for Basil to find even one.

"Don't you say his name."

Maribell choked down the last of the sleeping pills and stumbled from the bathroom. The hallway swam in her vision and she lurched against the wall. Behind her, the shadow thing stalked her. Silent. Waiting.

Her fingertips tingled and her feet lurched as if disconnected from her body. A fog descended, and she shook her head, trying to clear her thoughts. Basil's room. She had to reach Basil's room. Everything would be all right. She could fix this.

The floor rippled, and she pitched forward onto her knees.

Wordless, the dark creature urged her onward. She crawled over the threshold.

Moonlight streamed through the window. She didn't remember it getting dark. Dust motes danced in the beam, flashing like tiny, whirling stars. The train car bed, the overstuffed toy box, the sneakers with tangled laces faded from view. She had to cover the discolored spot on the rug, that one thing out of place in Basil's perfect sanctuary.

Maribell inched forward to curl across the damning stain, spotlighted by the moon's silver light. Her breath slowed. She'd just rest for a moment. As she closed her eyes, she noticed the carpet smelled like lemon-scented bleach.

The Vigil

Atop the bluff, salt-kissed wind slithered along the manor's rooftop and licked at the shingles. A few ruffled like feathers on a goose, but stayed in place with dogged tenacity. Ancient bones creaked as the timbers settled with a hunch-backed old man's complaints. A spray of rowan hung above the door, its protective aura fading as the berries withered and the dried leaves crumbled to dust. In contrast, sheltered by the chipped stone steps, a single primrose bloomed. In the gray lee of the moldering house, it made a splash of velvet purple with a miniature yellow sun at its heart.

Inside, the soul of the house—the Captain's wife—wandered from room to silent room. Embroidered silk slippers whispered over floorboards polished smooth by a hundred thousand footsteps. The manse shuddered at the uncanny tickle of a brùnaidh scampering in the walls, but the woman paid it no mind. The tiny feykin would get its due.

The library no longer held any secrets from the lady of the house, but she perused the titles, in case there was one she'd somehow not yet read. Leather and gilt and stiff parchment were old friends. The Captain preferred tales of adventure, like Fionn mac Cumhaill and his band of warriors. His wife returned again and again to the herbals and handwritten bestiaries. She'd scribbled notes in the margins: *Brùnaidh are helpful lil' housemates, but oft' offended. Ye'ken subdue a Kelpie with a halter stamped with a cross.* Little things people had forgotten, kept alive by her hand.

She double checked stoppered bottles of blue-black india ink and crimson dragon's blood and lined them up on the writing desk like rows of uniformed soldiers. The desk drawers held sheafs of creamy linen parchment and matching envelopes. A book of addresses sat unopened, filled with names of people who'd moved away and lost touch. She sharpened a quill, though she had no letters to write, and left it ready next to the ink before stepping out and closing the library door.

In the music room, the Captain's wife trailed her fingers over the old Bösendorfer piano. The ivory had yellowed with age, but the short keys remained glossy black. Pale, elegant hands danced in a complex series of chords with perfect execution, but the music seemed muted, as if the room had forgotten its resonance. The aria wove bittersweet notes, both exquisite and mournful. Then, the harmony grew sour. A shutter rattled against the window in arrhythmic accompaniment. Grimacing at the house's critique, she stepped away from the piano bench and moved on.

The drawing room felt lonely with the drapes closed and the hearth cold. Echoes of laughter and animated conversation lingered in the shadows, remnants of guests long departed. A draft carried the phantom scent of pipe smoke and brandy. Glasses clinked over the memory of deals being made, pleasant news shared. For a moment, the lady of the house thought she could see shapes—wispy shades of bygone years. She blinked, and they retreated into the past where they belonged.

Restless, she paced across the faded carpet. The room remained in perfect order, just as she last left it, unchanged but for the haunting whisper of days gone by. Rosewood furniture shined, any errant speck of dust polished away. The drink cart sat against the wall. It held pristine cut glass tumblers and decanters filled with expensive spirits. They waited in readiness for visitors that never came. Though the house staff had long since departed, the elusive brùnaidh took its housekeeping seriously. The Captain's wife repositioned a cushion that needed no straightening and left without a backward glance.

In the hall, the ornate grandfather clock struck the memory of seven. It no longer tick-tocked, but the sound was imprinted in her mind. She cocked her head and counted the phantom chimes that rang in the dinner hour. Out of habit, she drifted to the dining room, and a table set for one.

The Captain didn't believe in reserving the good dinnerware for company. Delicate china had arrived from the far east in a straw-packed crate. He'd presented it to her with a cheeky grin. The nearly transparent porcelain was hand painted with graceful lines and exotic flowers. She studied the plate and bowl before her and recalled how proud he had been to provide her with nice things. She looked at his empty seat at the head of the table and rubbed her chest, as if to ease the hollowness beneath her breastbone.

Like every night, she left the table without eating, for she had no appetite. Instead, she filled a bowl with cream and climbed the grand staircase to the solar. She kneeled by the unlit fireplace and set the offering down. Turning her back, she pretended to study a half-finished piece of needlework.

From the corner of her eye, she watched the brùnaidh slink from the shadows. The tiny house spirit had pointed ears and wore one of her thimbles for a cap. She forgave it for the theft. It was just nice to have the company. The brùnaidh lapped up the cream with greedy slurps, and she allowed herself an indulgent smile. Too many had forgotten the old lore, and the feykin faded. Not in her home. The manor sighed in agreement.

Leaving the creature to its dinner, she returned to the hall. Portraits lined the walls. Serious men with strong jawlines like the Captain and women wrapped in austere layers of lace and satin. They followed her with intense gazes, as if jealous she dared to move while they remained trapped in pigment and filigree frames.

Ignoring their gazes, the lady of the house peered through a series of doors, checking all was as it should be. Guest rooms that had seen no guests for years in one wing, the family quarters in the other. She hesitated at the Master suite. Behind the closed door lay a wardrobe filled with rainbow-hued ballgowns and her husband's patterned waistcoats. Her dressing table sat against one wall and a mahogany chiffonier against the other. Their vast four-poster bed waited with its fluffy feather tick.

When had she last slept?

The house creaked, and the door clicked open—inviting her to rest. She swept on by.

A hand pressed against her flat stomach, she squared her shoulders and peeked into the empty nursery. No memories haunted this place. Only the grief for what might-have-been thrived here, cut from her heart and taken up residence in the small room. The small space smelled of must and neglect, for even the brùnaidh dared not enter. The manor held her lament, the very walls of the nursery keeping her agony in its crumbling embrace. She closed the door, lest the darkness escape its confinement.

Her feet carried her onward, one last stop on her nightly rounds, before her new moon vigil would begin. The Captain's study.

She smoothed back maps and charts laid out on the round table. Reefs and tides and plotted stars, from the neighboring Orkney Islands to distant, exotic ports with unpronounceable names. She'd memorized them all. Would that she could pinpoint where he sailed now. She stared at the maps as if a red X would appear in answer to her questions and her prayers. She rubbed gritty eyes and turned away.

Trinkets and baubles from her husband's travels decorated the room. A silk tapestry depicting a serpentine, whiskered dragon. A golden statue, no larger than her splayed palm, that waved a dozen arms. The claw from a manticore that hung from a frayed hemp cord. Behind it, the wainscoting twisted, as if the manor shrank away from the foreign magic. She patted the wall in agreement. Scottish lore, like the brùnaidh and the kelpie, was in her blood, but the wicked talon radiated an otherness that did not belong here.

She sat at her husband's desk and tried to envision him writing in his logbook or tallying his ledgers, tongue between his teeth as he calculated his profits. Her stomach curdled. His scent had faded—spice, tobacco, and the ever-present taste of the sea—remembered but no longer perfuming the air. She fiddled with the tarnished astrolabe before her. When she'd realized he'd forgotten it, she'd sprinted down to the shore, but his ship had already sailed. If only she had run faster, would he be sitting here now?

The window rattled, shattering her reverie. Outside, the sun sank into the sea, the sky painted mauve and lilac. The window shook again.

"All right, me ol' friend. Ah'm gooin.'"

She gathered up an empty lantern and glided to the end of the hall. With a steady step, she climbed a narrow set of stairs. She needed no light to guide her. One by one, she counted the risers until she reached the top and ducked out onto the widow's walk.

A sea breeze toyed with her hair as she looked down at the waters far below. A pair of selkies played in the surf. She imagined, even from this distance, she could hear the slaps of their tails and see their twitching whiskers. One paused and looked up at her with dark, liquid eyes. The villagers called them seals, but she knew when the moon was full they'd come ashore and shed their pelts to walk on two legs, for she used to join them on the pebbled beach. The joy it brought to walk among them, to listen to their songs, and to draw her own bone comb through their long tresses. She missed their companionship, but she no longer left the house. The selkies dived beneath the surface and disappeared.

Above her the shingles rustled, although the wind had died. She glanced up. Tonight there was no moon. In the darkness, any ship navigating the reefs would crash against the rocky shore before it realized it came close. She imagined her brave husband, drifting beneath the waves, bloated and pale.

The house whispered in her ear—*nay on our watch*.

She nodded. Nay on our watch.

The Captain's wife chanted, a lilting song that blended with the roar of the surf and the chime of starlight. Fingers traced arcane symbols in the air. The night held its breath until a pair of lights appeared. They hovered above her head, diving and flashing. The tinkle of crystalline laughter sounded in her ears.

"Come now, dearies." She coaxed the will-o'-the-wisps into the lantern. "Just for the long, dark night, me loves." The lights danced inside the glass globe. "I'll free ye in the morn' and naught call again 'til the moon grows dark once more."

The will-o'-the-wisps twinkled with an uncanny glow. She hung the lantern on a hook. Behind her, tin and mercury-lined glass reflected the light, a beacon in the night.

The Captain's wife leaned on the rail and stared out into the boundless sea. Together, she and the ancient manor kept their vigil. Waiting for their lord to come home.

#

Aidan pulled his bike up short. "Callum! I ken it!" He pointed at the decaying mansion on the top of the cliff. "Do ye see?"

Callum squinted. Up on the widow's walk, a light shone in the night. He sucked in his breath between the gap in his front teeth with a whistle. "Wit is it?"

"T'is the Dark Widow. They say her husband was lost at sea a 'undred years ago. She lights a lantern on the new moon ta shepard him home."

Callum shivered. "Bollocks. There's nae such thing as ghosts."

"Then 'splain the light." Aidan grinned. "Legend has it, the Widow is the heart of the house, and iffin she gives up her vigil the manor'll collapse!"

"Ye're aff yer heid! I heard the house gets a cream delivery."

"But nae groceries." Aidan wrinkled his brow, working it out. "She could hae a wee broonie she's feedin'!"

"Don't be daft. Ghosts that feed fairy folk? Next ting y'll be tellin' me ye believe in selkies and loch monsters."

From out on the sea a bell tolled.

Callum looked at Aidan, eyes suddenly wide. "And what's spose'ta happen when the Captain returns?" He pointed a shaking hand toward the waves.

In the bay, a translucent clipper ship emerged from an eerie fog and trimmed her sails. A dozen ghostly forms manned the sweeps. The trader slipped across the waters, leaving no wake, a silent relic of yesteryear. A deep voice echoed in the night.

"Land ho!" It made the hair on the back of Callum's neck stand on end.

Atop the bluff, the old manor house rippled, and the boys saw it as it had been a century before. The shingles straightened, the paint looked bright and fresh. The weeds disappeared, and meticulous gardens encircled the house, lush with night-blooming flowers and medicinal herbs. Candles shone from every window, sparkling like fireflies.

The thick oak door, carved with dozens of creatures, swung open and a woman in an old-fashioned, flowing gown stepped out on the porch. Her raven locks spilled loose across her shoulders and tears glistened on her cheeks. She hesitated, reaching up to touch the bright orange berries on the rowan branch pinned to the lintel. As she started down the stairs, the two boys glanced at each other and held their breaths.

Under the star-speckled sky, the Captain's wife squared her shoulders and, for the first time in a hundred years, left the shelter of the house.

Chameleon

I used to vacation at the beach in February for the solitude. Now it's always winter. Still, I stay at this forgotten cottage by the shore, because at least being constantly alone feels familiar here. For all I know, I'm all that's left, anywhere.

They prefer to hunt in the dark, and since *They* shattered the moon, there's only high tide and higher. The sand is hard beneath my feet. I've stopped looking for seashells. Any bit of sea life left has retreated into the deep. It's as if even the sand dollars and mollusks know that *They* are ravenous.

I glance at the sky. A burnt-orange haze stretches to the horizon. Pink and crimson no longer announce the day's end, but I should have an hour before the hidden sun sets. A few more moments before I must turn around to make it home before full dark. If I hurry, I can reach the point. It's farther than I've gone before, but something drives my feet onward. I study the sky again, and walk on.

Ahead, a small pile of rocks catches my attention. Tucked into the side of the dune, it's perched just above the "higher" tide mark. I look up and down the beach, but see nothing but miles of surf-flattened, empty sand.

I approach the pile, thinking it looks like a stone cairn, then shake the dark thought from my head. It's just a stack of fist-sized rocks, jumbled haphazardly together.

Except, it's not.

I reach for the top stone. Hoarfrost rims the flat edges. Cold burns through my gloves, stings my fingers. Blood roars in my ears, in rhythm with the waves. Across the rock's sand-polished surface, a single word is scrawled in an uneven, childlike hand.

hELo?

I study the pile. Each rock bears the same word, written in faded marker. A lump grows in my throat. The stones remind me of the art project I used to do with my kindergarten classes. Messages in bottles or painted on rocks, tiny wooden signs and bits of colorful ceramics, all hidden around the city, their uplifting messages meant to cheer a downtrodden community. Back in a time when I thought random encouragement from strangers could make a difference. Would be welcomed, even.

My eyes water. I rub them before my eyelashes freeze together.

When my vision clears, I notice my shadow is too long. I stuff the rock into my pocket and go. I have to sprint the final yards to get back to my little beach cottage before dark. Slamming the door behind me, my heart thunders in my chest. Foolish risk. The night belongs to *Them*.

#

My stomach growls as I settle cross legged on the floor to wait out the night. There wasn't time to open one of the dwindling supply of canned goods. I pretend I'm not hungry; that I'm deliberately rationing—not giving into the fear of moving around in the dark.

Keeping my actions small, I strip off my gloves and pull the rock from my pocket. I cradle it in my hands. My fingers learn the cool, polished curves, trace the letters. I can't see or feel them, but I know they're there. My jacket rustles and I freeze.

No light. No sound. No movement.

That's how I've survived *Their* pitch black hunting hours. Or so I tell myself.

Maybe *They* are gone. Packed up their ships and moved on to devour some other world. Why cast a line when there's only one fish left to catch? I remain silent and still. Just in case *They're* nearby and hungry. Of course, *They* are. *They're* always hungry and the night is very long.

When the gap around the curtains lightens, I stretch out and fall into a fitful sleep. I dream of roaring traffic, shouting children, and barking dogs. The press of crowds on the sidewalk. A honking cab. The constant roar of noise that used to be my norm.

I jerk awake. My instinct is to reach for the phone, muscle memory that urges me to dial my sister, Dani. I want to tell her about my dreams and the stone cairn. She always gives clever advice. Silence presses in on me as I remember she stopped answering long before the lines went dead. I tell myself it doesn't mean anything. She could be hunkered down somewhere, spending her nights quiet and still, just like me.

My fingers cramp, still clutching the rock. I peel open my hand and study the faded letters. Who left the message? How long ago? The mystery has me lacing up my boots and heading back down the beach.

Urgency lends my feet speed. I make better time than yesterday and soon see the stacked rocks in the distance. It seems larger than before. No, I'm sure I'm misremembering. Solitude plays tricks on the mind, and I've been alone for longer than I can remember.

I reach the pile and a shiver, like an icy serpent, slithers down my spine. New rocks are piled atop the old, their magic-markered messages bold and dark.

iS SomE onE ThErE?

hElo?

Im lonEly.

Hello?

The handwriting becomes clearer, more refined with each message. A child, growing up too quickly.

Are you there?

On the top rock, the scrawl matures into a tidy script with a familiar looping flourish on the y's tail.

Tracey?

Dani has always had such lovely handwriting. Mine looks like chicken scratch in comparison. Ironic that she is the doctor and I, the artist. She loves saying our talents got tangled up as children since we spent all our time together. Sisters and best friends. The echo of her laugh dances in my head like a pale sun reflecting ice chip sparks on a winter sea.

I tear myself from the memory. Even if she's not gone, she's out of reach, leaving me hollowed out and alone. I look down at the rock in my hand. The message in her handwriting screams at me. I drop it, as if it's a burning ember.

They are master chameleons, sifting through our thoughts and plucking out our memories, so *Their* blank, egg-like faces can shift into perfect replicas of our family and friends. By the time we figured it out, it was too late, *They* had nearly devoured us all.

I kick over the stones and dash down the beach. Staying close to the water's edge, I let the frigid waves wash away my footprints in the sand. My toes grow numb. If *They* are hunting, I will not be easy prey.

Inside the cabin, I shove the old, sun-bleached loveseat against the back door. I double check the window locks. I check again.

I wish for more furniture to block the front door too, but make do with the deadbolt and chain. I burned the tables and chairs in the early days. Back when I felt safer out here on this lonely strip of beach and the need for keeping warm outweighed the fear. Back when there were crowded cities for *Them* to hunt in.

There is nothing left to do but wait. Overhead, burnt-orange slowly transitions to shadows. The minutes pass, long as hours, in the quiet night. For an unknown eternity, I let myself almost believe there's nothing stalking down the dark beach, searching for one last meal.

The porch step creaks.

A knock comes at the door, soft and hesitant.

"Tracey?" Dani's voice trembles. "Let me in. I'm so tired. I walked all the way here."

The knocking grows more insistent.

"Please. *They* are coming."

Her terror sounds real. She sounds real.

I bury my face in my hands and pray I am wrong.

Cake

My world was off-kilter, senses skewed.

The afternoon sun blazed liquid gold across the robin's egg sky. Along the riverbank, the sugar maples wore crimson buds. Even the dark water reflected a kaleidoscope of Springtime hues.

I shook my head. The rainbow seemed washed out, like a sun-bleached photograph.

In the canopy above, a pair of sparrows chirped a lively serenade. A bullfrog, nestled in the muddy embankment, harmonized in a deep baritone. The breeze whispered through the treetops. Mother Nature conducted a riverside symphony.

It sounded discordant in my ears, and I shivered as if icy fingertips tickled my spine.

Dangling my feet over the edge of the dock, I wrapped one arm around the piling. If I pointed my toes they'd skim the water's surface. I didn't dare. Checking my watch, I swung my legs back and forth and waited for her to arrive. I didn't have to wait for long.

The frog leaped into the river with a faint plop. A cloud passed over the sun and the wind died. The birds fell silent. Huddled together on their branch, they fluffed up their feathers and watched with wary eyes.

"You shouldn't keep calling me to meet you here." She settled down next to me, close but not touching.

The hairs on the back of my neck stood up and I pulled my sweatshirt close. I hadn't heard her approach.

"I know, Mom. I just miss talking with you." Eyes downcast, I refused to look at her.

"Oh, darling." Her voice quivered. "I do too."

Now that she was here all the words I'd been desperate to say bottled up in my throat. I fixed my gaze on the river below my feet. On the surface, it appeared calm, but the water was deep and the current swift. Dangerous territory.

"Out with it, then. What's bothering you?"

"It's *her* birthday." I picked at the hem of my sleeve, refusing to call my stepmother by her name. Not in front of my real mom. "Dad's throwing her a party."

"Love isn't finite. Caring for her won't diminish what you feel for me." She chuckled. "Besides, parties mean cake." Her laugh trailed off with the suggestion of a gurgle. "I miss cake."

My face flushed as a wave of anger swept over me. "It's not fair." I blinked hard, refusing to cry. "I just wish it could go back to the way things were."

"I wish that too." Water dripped down the piling, the individual drops swallowed up and swept away. "But you can't change what happened."

Thinking about that day twisted my stomach in knots. The fragmented images jumped in my memory, disjointed like a scratched DVD. A loud crack as the wood splintered. The shock of the freezing water. Arms and legs thrashed, turned heavy. Lungs burned. Panic.

Darkness.

It took four days for my body to learn to breathe on its own again. When I woke, I drowned anew. This time in guilt.

"I see your father fixed the dock." Her voice pulled me from the memory.

I unballed my fingers from my sleeve and touched the wood between us. Two unpainted planks showed sharp contrast to the darker, weathered ones on either side.

"Yeah. *She* likes to kayak and has asked me to come with her a few times. Said it might be good for me, but..." I trailed off. Fists clenched, my nails dug into my palms.

The silence stretched as she waited for me to finish.

"I'm so sorry, Momma." I choked the words out over a sob.

"Sweetheart, it was an accident." She cleared her throat. "I saved you." A coughing fit stole her words. I held my breath until she could continue. "I'd do it again. A million times over."

I stared at my hands.

"Look at me, baby." She used her 'mom voice.' The one that brooked no argument.

I forced myself to turn my head. Her skin was pallid, lips tinged blue. Ropes of dripping hair clung to her face like auburn seaweed. Water trickled from her nose. Her green eyes, twin to my own, clouded over with a milky film. She flickered as if she were pulled elsewhere. Somehow, I knew my remorse tethered her. I didn't want her to move on. Shame swamped me.

She reached a translucent hand toward me, fingers hovering inches above my arm. Regret crossed her face as she pulled back and folded her hands in her lap. I wished she would touch me, just once.

"Loving your stepmom isn't betraying me." She said it gently, but it still stung. "I just want you and your dad to be happy."

I scrubbed the back of my hand over my eyes.

"You have to let me go." Her 'mom voice' was back. "Enjoy the party. Eat the cake."

The clouds parted and a ray of sunshine fell on her. For a moment I saw her as she had been—long frizzy curls framed by smooth rosy cheeks. Her eyes twinkled and the corners of her pink lips curled up in the hint of a smile. "I hope it's chocolate."

The words sounded like goodbye.

I blinked and she was gone.

A breeze teased my hair, and I tucked the stray waves behind my ear. The treetops chattered as the branches rubbed together and the sparrows resumed their chorus. I scrambled to my feet. If I didn't hurry, I'd be late for the party.

The Vast Enormity of the Sea

Cold, quiet, dark. That's what I told landlubbers when they asked what diving was like. What I didn't say was how peaceful it was, especially the deeper I went. Just me and my thoughts and a passing eel or two.

I checked my depth gauge. Forty meters. Glancing up, I located my spotter. He hovered near the oil rig's massive metal leg about three meters above me—making an inky, finned silhouette in the darkness, an odd merman illuminated by the fading spotlight of his headlamp. I circled my forefinger and thumb, holding up my other three fingers in an *a-okay* gesture. He flipped me the bird. Not technically on the list of the Diver's Association's official hand signals.

Being the crew's underwater welder—the highest-paid diver on the rig—was one thing. The gall of holding that position as a woman was something else altogether. It hadn't made me a whole lot of drinking buddies.

Shrugging, I got back to work. I was an excellent welder, a better diver, and didn't need some asshole spotter to keep me safe.

#

My sheets are wet. Not night sweat damp, but cold and sopping. Despite the chill, I can't make myself move, only listen to the rhythmic plink-plonk of water dripping onto the floor. My brain struggles to understand what my body feels. How could someone dump an entire bucket of water on the bed and not wake me?

This is one prank too far. I've ignored the never-ending parade of half-rotten fish heads in my boots. I don't complain that somehow, I always get the gritty dregs of the coffee at breakfast. Screwing with my sleep, though, is the last straw. Diving tired makes you shark bait.

Still in my sodden pajamas, I stalk down the hall, leaving a trail of wet footprints behind me. When I reach the Toolpusher's cabin, I bang on the door. He's a mouse of a man, but surely, he'll do something. It's his rig to manage, his crew to wrangle.

He doesn't answer the door.

Coward.

I return to my bunk, but when I bend to strip the bedding, I realize it's dry. Is this part of the joke? It makes little sense. I flop down on the hard mattress, annoyed but too exhausted to do much else. Something pokes me in the shoulder. I fish around in the sheets and pull out a shell the size of a ping-pong ball. Not the wave-beaten, fractured bit of calcite that people oh and ah over on white sand beaches, but a fully spiraled nautilus.

My thoughts, fuzzy in that liminal space between waking and sleep, do not dwell on how such a thing ended up in my bed, but rather that I hope the critter who lived inside has moved out. I imagine the feel of tiny appendages on my cheek.

I'm sure it's all a dream.

#

Something brushed the back of my leg, softly but firm enough I could feel it through my dry suit. Amateur divers panicked, thrashing and churning in the water when the ocean reached out and touched them. Just like prey. Experienced divers stayed calm. And alive.

Without looking down, I flipped off the welding iron. Four hundred amps of direct current screamed through the electrode, and I had no interest in getting fried. Wet welding was far more dangerous than anything the ocean might tickle me with.

I blinked and double-checked the weld. Straight and even. I gave a thumbs up to my spotter and he reeled in the equipment. The jerk didn't bother to wait for me, but fins churning, swam straight up toward the first decompression stop. His light faded to a pinprick, then nothingness.

Another touch drew my attention. Slow and calm, I turned, bringing my headlamp around. A grayish-pink tentacle felt up my leg, gentle suckers exploring the seam in my dry suit. The octopus was massive, with arms thicker than my thigh. My heart thudded in my ears. Another enormous tentacle wrapped around my waist.

I shuddered and reminded myself that octopuses were smart and curious, rarely aggressive to humans.

It pulled me closer until I was face to face with a dinner plate sized eye.

For the first time, I understood how sailors of old began rumors of the Kraken.

#

Everything tastes like brine, even the coffee. I grimace and set the mug down. Something wriggles in my bowl of stew. I look closer. A swarm of sea fleas backstroke in the broth and feast on the lumps of over-salted beef. I shove the bowl away, trying not to throw up.

I look around to see if anyone else notices the rancid food. The mess hall is nearly deserted, with only a handful of serious-faced diners sitting close together and whispering in low voices. No one looks at me. Fine. It's better than the sneers and scowls that usually come my way.

Everything's oddly quiet. I can feel the sway of the platform and the never-ceasing hum of the drilling equipment, but it's as if there's water in my ears. I tilt my head to the side, like an overgrown retriever, and hop, trying to shake the water out.

I've never had a dog. I figure I travel too much, and it wouldn't be fair for it to be always waiting for me to come home. It's a bit of a dream, though, for retirement. People like me either retire early, bodies too beat up to keep working, or die on the job. My knees ache and I'm banking on early retirement.

Meal forgotten, I pick up my phone and scroll through pet adoption websites, getting goo-goo-eyed over the labs and pitties and mutts, trying to make an impossible choice. Which do I get when my contract is up? They're all perfect—they don't judge or demand anything but belly rubs.

A shadow falls across the table.

"Perhaps you'd be better off adopting a sea lion." The unfamiliar voice bubbles and slurps like the speaker has a mouth full of water. "They're like puppies of the ocean, you know."

#

One of the Kraken's tentacles—I no longer thought of it as a mere octopus—prodded at my air tank. I attempted to peel the strong arm back as it fiddled with the knobs, but couldn't budge it. A boulder dropped into my stomach. I tried to wiggle out of the creature's grasp. Its sharp beak snapped at me.

I froze.

A voice in my head screamed at me to fight; kick and slash until I was free. I inched my hand toward the hilt of the dive knife in my belt. Again, the beak snapped, barely missing my fingers, as if it knew my intention.

I forced my muscles to relax, knowing the creature could feel my tension. I told myself everything was okay. It was just curious about the odd, two-legged swimming mammal. I was fine. Fine. Fine. Finefinefine. The words ran together in my head until they held no meaning.

Another sinuous limb skated up my body in a lover's caress, across my chest, up my shoulder, flirting touches on my neck. Suckers kissed and popped over my jaw, along my cheek. The beast knocked my mask askew, and water rushed in, salt stinging my eyes. My vision blurred.

#

The man draws out a chair and sits across from me. A bloodless gash runs up the side of his face, from jaw to temple. The edges of the cut are tinged blue, stark against his too-pale skin. His hair and beard are long, matted locks of gray kelp. Water pours from his clothes—a tattered, old-fashioned nautical uniform as if he's an extra on some pirate movie set. Murky puddles grow on the floor.

A crab emerges from his collar and scuttles down his arm. He seems not to notice. Perhaps for him, it is commonplace for sea creatures to roam around in his clothes. I try not to stare, for fear of being rude.

He helps himself to my coffee, swallowing it down with a great thirst. Brown liquid seeps from the gouge on his cheek.

"I miss coffee." His voice still sounds water-garbled, but I find it easy to understand. "And ale." He looks around wistfully, then picks up my phone, dripping salt water on the screen.

I want to tell him to return to the sea. Drowned men have no place here, drinking coffee and surfing the web. I can't form the words, for my tongue feels thick and swollen in my mouth.

"So, as I was saying, don't sign the adoption papers just yet." He points at a blocky pittie mix, with a stubby tail and brown-tipped ears. "Too bad, though. This one is pretty cute."

#

A beep sounded, insistent in my ear. The depth gauge flashed.

Sixty meters.

Eighty-five.

The Kraken pulled me deeper. I wondered if my spotter was still at the decompression station, wondering why I hadn't joined him. Or had it been five minutes already and had he gone on? If he leapfrogged ahead to the next pause, he'd never know I wasn't following one stop behind.

His lack of protocol was going to kill me. I should have tried harder to be friends instead of proving to everyone I was strong and capable. I am woman, hear me roar...and all that bullshit. Hubris was just as likely to make a waterlogged corpse out of me.

I struggled, legs thrashing. Tentacles hugged me tighter, like a fly wrapped in a spider's web. My breath came too fast, and I sucked air through the regulator until I was close to hyperventilating, no regard to the level of reserves.

Again, the gauge beeped. It sounded lethargic and tired.

A hundred and fifty meters. I wondered how deep the creature could dive.

Which was worse? Crushing or drowning?

#

The old sailor and I speak for hours, for days, for a small eternity.

He tells me of his wife, with raven hair and ice-chip eyes. She waited, haunting the widow's walk, staring at an empty sea. He wonders if she still waits, a specter on a seaside rooftop praying to see a sail emerge from beyond the horizon.

"When you give yourself to the sea," he says, "you make peace with the idea that you might never come home. That no one will ever really know what happened to you. At least there was someone there waiting for me. Hoping, you know?"

He gives me a sad smile.

"Sorry 'bout that. It could have been the dog for you." He taps my phone screen again. "You shouldn't have waited to bring this little feller home."

I rub at the hollow ache in my chest and change the subject. "Will it hurt? When my lungs explode." I'm curious, not afraid.

He pats my hand as if I'm a child who has asked a very silly question.

#

The Kraken made the decision.

Drowning.

The tentacle cupping my face ripped the regulator from my mouth. My mind knew I shouldn't scream, but my body did it anyway. Seawater rushed in.

It should have been cold, but it burned. For a moment.

As my heartbeat slowed, regret prickled like the sting of fire coral. There was no one to wait for me, to long for my return. Not even a dog.

The thought slipped away until there was nothing left but an empty void. Then the void filled with the vast enormity of the sea. It turned me inside out, sucking away warmth and light, those wicked tormentors of hope. In its place, there was only tranquility.

I never told people how peaceful diving was. In that magnificent stillness, deep below the surface, I welcomed the cold, quiet, dark.

Not Quite Finished

Aimee swirled her paintbrush in the muddy glass of water, then dabbed it on a paper towel. Turning back to the canvas, she studied what she'd painted. A terraced mountainside, the exposed cliff faces rich in browns and oranges and yellows. At the top, a wide plateau stretched into the distance, covered in green scrub brush. Every detail seemed perfect, a moment frozen in time. She could almost feel the grainy soil beneath her feet. A mischievous wind tousled her hair. The scent of sage and sunbaked rock filled her nose.

Looking closer, she could see two tiny figures scrambling along one of the narrow earthen platforms. She frowned.

I don't remember painting that.

A fine line ran between the two forms, tethered together by a rope. Aimee narrowed her eyes, trying to take in the details. The smaller figure had a blonde ponytail. The taller wore a checkered shirt.

Nope. I definitely didn't paint that.

Aimee glanced at the array of paintbrushes on her worktable. She didn't have the tools or the talent for such tiny detail work. Broad, bold strokes were more her forte. Her hand trembled, and she clenched it into a fist.

When her gaze returned to the painting, the figures had moved. The man had climbed halfway up the face of the next level. He clung, spiderlike, one arm extended to the woman. His hand beckoned her to join him. She had one foot poised to climb. A faint whisper scratched at Aimee's ears—the phantom encouragement of an experienced climber, coaching his partner on where to put her feet.

She shook her head, face flushed.

This is too weird.

Standing, she went into the kitchen and poured herself a glass of water. For a moment, she held it against her hot cheek, enjoying the feel of the condensation against her skin. She made a mental note to ask the super to check the air conditioning. It rumbled and hummed, but the air felt sweltering.

Feeling a little better, she went back to her studio to clean up. She tried to ignore the painting but stole quick glances out of the corner of her eye as she worked. Like a stop-motion flipbook, the two small rock climbers worked their way towards the top of the mountain, moving in those moments she wasn't looking. Her breath caught in her throat as the woman's foot slipped. Aimee tore her gaze away.

At her next peek, a frozen deluge of rocks and dirt tumbled down the terraces. She clamped a hand over her eyes. Her heart pounded in her chest as she listened to the miniature avalanche roar in her head.

Silence fell, and she forced herself to look. Both figures had made the next ledge. They lay flat on their backs, hands clasped together. Painted on canvas, they did not move, but Aimee could sense the feeling of chests heaving. Gasping breath turned to relief, becoming manic, unbridled laughter. She could hear its ghostly echo, like the memory of a film watched years ago, details muted by time. The hairs on the back of her neck stood on end.

This is ridiculous.

She grabbed a brush and loaded it with a blob of cinnamon-colored paint.

Swipe, swish, dab.

Three strokes and the two invaders disappeared. She blew on the paint, willing it to dry, then added another layer for security. Sometimes a single coat couldn't hide what lay beneath. Though she could not see them, she imagined the figures squirmed beneath her brush.

I wonder if it tickles?

She pushed the thought aside, cleaned the brushes, and packed the paint away. Enough art for one day. She drew a hot bath and poured a glass of wine.

Exactly what I need.

One glass of wine became two. She felt restless, like there was something that needed finishing. She checked her calendar, her messages; opened the washer to make sure she hadn't forgotten to switch a load. She fed the fish until they stopped swimming to the surface and simply hovered in the bowl, fat and lethargic. She finished the bottle of wine and went to bed, plagued by fractured dreams.

The next morning, her head ached and her tongue felt covered in cotton. Struggling out of bed, she followed her feet as they led her back into her studio.

What the hell?

The figures were back, right at the top of the mountain, climbing the final leg. Clinging to the sheer rock face, the woman's mouth stretched open in a silent scream. The man dangled from the rope between them, arms windmilling and flannel shirt askew.

Aimee rubbed her eyes. The flip book changed.

The man's eyes were wide in his face. He'd tried to find a handhold, but had swung too far from the wall.

He's too heavy for her. They'll both fall.

A minuscule glint of silver reflected in the woman's hand. She held it to the rope. Aimee's fingers spasmed, clenching a phantom hilt.

Stomach roiling, Aimee looked away.

She could still feel the tension on the rope and the way it had given way under her hands. Damon had screamed as he fell. The base of the mountain was too far away to hear when he landed, but she'd imagined the crunch of bone.

Stop. This isn't real.

She counted a hundred Mississippis, waiting for her thumping heart to slow. Gathering her resolve about her like a fluffy blanket, she looked back at the painting. The figures were gone. As if they'd never been.

Not quite finished.

In a daze, she rummaged through the tubes of paint until she found the right one. Carefully, she selected her finest brush. She surveyed the base of the mountain, looking for the perfect spot. Her hand knew exactly where to dab a small splat of paint.

Horrified, she studied what she'd created. The crimson pool of blood soaked the ground, just as she remembered it.

Now it's done.

The Fear Liath

Like one, that on a lonesome road
doth walk in fear and dread,
and having once turned round walks on,
and turns no more his head;
because he knows, a frightful fiend
doth close behind him tread.
Samuel Taylor Coleridge—Rime of the Ancient Mariner (1834)

\#

Words flickered across a control panel in a line of obnoxiously cheerful green text:

FIVE SECONDS TO LAUNCH.

Five measly seconds before they flung Norm's pod into a wyrmhole. Nowhere near long enough for a person to ready themselves for the ordeal. Ten more seconds before he and the ball of titanium-epoxy resin HQ called a spacecraft were shot out of the ball return. A quick round of pinball was how they'd explained it with a laugh and a clap on his shoulder.

The reality was far worse.

For a sliver of eternity, his mind and body separated, neither *here* nor *there*, but inexplicably both, before rejoining with a whole-body whiplash. Norm gave silent thanks for the snug restraints. He was a software developer, not a damned spaceman.

When they'd asked him to take an interplanetary quick-jump pod up to Am Liath Mòr in order to "fix" TerraPro—his proprietary terraforming software—he should've refused. Onsite support wasn't in his contract. Besides, users were the worst, always blaming the program for their own incompetence. The code was impeccable. He should know; he'd written it. Yet, somehow, he'd found himself on this ridiculous transport on his way to a light-forsaken, tumbleweed-ridden corner of the universe to hold the hands of a bunch of idiotic planet hackers incapable of figuring out a basic user interface.

PREPARE FOR DOCKING.

Norm dismissed the internal rant. Too late for regrets; he was already here.

As the pod connected to the orbiting Nexus Control Station with a gentle thump, he unclipped, stood, and shook his limbs to work out the pins and needles. There was no way he was going to embarrass himself in front of the crew, bumbling around like a travel-sick weakling, so he took his time before disembarking. Once settled, he squared his shoulders, then entered the command codes on the airlock's keypad.

Damn plant-jumper pod didn't even have voice commands. He rolled his eyes.

A hissing filled the cabin as the pressure equalized. When it stopped, the bulkhead slid open, and he stepped out onto the station's deck.

Norm took a deep breath. The air felt thin and icy. He sucked it in, but his lungs were lead balloons, impossible to inflate. His head swam. Staggering into the control center, he aimed for an orderly bank of consoles. Black dots spotted his vision, like bugs crawling across a screen. Numb fingers fumbled across the keyboard as he brought up life support—nineteen percent and dropping. Gasping, he reset the system.

Vents whooshed. The air warmed.

For a moment, all he could do was breathe.

Norm's knees wobbled, and he collapsed in a chair, blinking at the screen, his oxygen-starved brain struggling to make sense of the log history. The life support system hadn't failed. Someone had turned it down.

The hairs on the back of his neck prickled.

Glancing around, he realized the command center was empty. Where the hell was the crew? This project was supposed to be big doings—slated to be the newest luxury resort planet for the rich and famous. He'd expected bustling activity as the high-powered computers directed robotic terraforming operations on the planet's surface below. Instead, he found rows of empty seats and dark consoles.

Why'd he bother making the trip if no one was even here to meet him? He scowled. The thought of the sabotaged life support system turned the scowl into a grimace.

Something moved in his peripherals.

Norm turned as a shadow slipped out into the hallway. He struggled to his feet and followed, still a touch dizzy. The indistinct shape disappeared around the corner with the oiled grace of a serpent.

"Hello? Anyone there? I'm Norm Collie. HQ sent me. You know, the Programmer?" The words ricocheted off the bulkheads in a ghostly parody of his voice.

Helllloo? Norm Collieeeee. The Programmmmmmmmer?

He shivered.

"Someone's got to be here." This time he spoke more quietly, to avoid the magpie spectral-echo.

Down the hall, he explored the living quarters, finding them deserted. Personal items remained in the bunks, but no sign of life. At the end of the corridor, the dim mess hall also had an eerie, recently abandoned air. The chairs were askew and, here and there, crumbs decorated the tabletops where someone had forgotten to wipe them up after eating. It felt lived in, but empty, as if he'd just missed dinner.

The longer Norm poked around, the more the feeling he wasn't truly alone grew. His skin crawled with the weight of an unseen gaze. He searched the room. A menacing form, a shade of charcoal somewhat darker than the gray shadows, lurked in the corner. Vaguely man-shaped, it loomed too tall and impossibly thin to be a crew member.

He shrank back, bumping against a table.

"Lights: one hundred percent." His voice shook so hard he had to give the command a second time before the computer acknowledged.

Bright, sterile white chased the shadows away. Norm let out an anemic chuckle and leaned against the table, knees weak. The corner was empty. He rubbed his eyes, trying to shake off the aftereffects of the low oxygen. What an idiot. He was glad there had been no one there to see his silliness.

Still, where *was* everyone? Maybe the logs would have answers.

When he headed back down the hall, something clomped in rhythm behind him.

He paused. The footsteps paused.

Glancing over his shoulder, he saw nothing but a lonely corridor of unadorned, generic metal. No one followed. He shrugged the sound off as his own treads, reverbing off the walls. The damn echo again. Setting his shoulders against the urge to run, he refused to look again, even when the footsteps once again paced close behind.

"There's nothing there. Nothing."

The echo reassured him. *NothingNothingnothingnothing.*

Unconvinced, his pulse thrummed in time to the staccato footsteps. Hot air fluttered against the back of his neck, the fetid breath of some creature stalking prey. He spun around and backpedaled, arms windmilling.

A long shadow stretched across the metal floor, cast from nothing. The stretched-taffy shape pulsed, as if taking in a slow breath, then letting it out again. In. Out. In. Out.

A moan built in Norm's throat, stoppered by his tongue.

He took a step back.

The shadow creature followed in lockstep.

Norm's trapped moan escaped as a feeble whimper.

Though the creature had no face, it projected a vague sense of a smile, imagined fangs glinting in the pulsing darkness.

Norm took another step back, but his feet tangled together. He reached out to steady himself on the wall. When he looked up, the shadow was gone, like fog burned off by morning sunlight.

He shook off the absurd thoughts. Shadow creatures, indeed. Still, he inched backwards down the rest of the hallway, not taking his eyes off the spot where the darkness had been, unwilling to give his back to the nonexistent monster.

By the time he reached the computer lab, he began to relax. The taunting echo-steps had fallen silent. No weird shadows stalked the corridors. He sighed as he settled behind a console and the tension slipped from his muscles—the hum of computers and strings of code were his comfort zone. Tapping the keyboard, he pulled up the Crew Foreman's log.

AUTHORIZATION REQUIRED.

Norm grinned. "Not for me, sweetheart." He keyed in the override commands.

TERRAFORMING IS STALLED. THE INITIAL SURFACE TOPOGRAPHY OF AM LIATH MÒR HAS BEEN SUCCESSFULLY MODIFIED, BUT THE PLANET REMAINS UNSUITABLE FOR INTRODUCING ATMOSPHERE SHAPING PLANTS. DESPITE NUMEROUS ATTEMPTS TO RESET PARAMETERS TO CONTINUE SOIL MODIFICATIONS, TERRAPRO IS BUGGY. SENT A REQUEST TO HQ FOR A SITE VISIT FROM THE PROGRAMMER.

Buggy. Norm glowered and dug into the code. He ran diagnostics, searched for viruses. Everything came up clean. As he suspected—user error. He harrumphed and rolled his eyes. It was always user error.

Still, it didn't explain where everyone had disappeared to. Goosebumps pebbled his arms as he read on.

FEAR AND PARANOIA ARE SPREADING. SIGHTINGS OF A STRANGE "GRAYMAN" HAVE BEEN CONFIRMED

SHIP WIDE. REPORTS DESCRIBE THE GRAYMAN AS BIPEDAL, ROUGHLY HUMANOID, APPROX. 3M TALL, GAUNT, WITH DARK, WILD HAIR. CHECKED AIR FILTERS FOR HALLUCINOGENIC MOLD AND FOOD REPLICATORS FOR MALFUNCTIONS. NEGATIVE. NO REASONABLE EXPLANATION CAN BE ATTRIBUTED TO THE SIGHTINGS.

A whisper came from the hall, rhythmic like faint breathing. Norm shuddered with the sense of endless cockroaches scurrying up his spine. He double checked the door and the empty corridor. After verifying he truly was alone, he shook his head and returned to the log. The need to figure out what had happened and to get the hell off the station intensified.

OFF-SHIP COMMUNICATIONS DOWN.

1318: CREWMAN WILSON REPORTED A GRAYMAN SIGHTING; THE THIRD ONE THIS REVOLUTION.

1437: AGAINST ORDERS, WILSON COMMANDEERED AN ESCAPE POD. 100M FROM THE DOCKING PORT, THE POD EXPLODED. IT WAS THE FINAL REMAINING EVACUATION OPTION.

THE CREW IS FRANTIC, AND GRAYMAN SIGHTINGS ARE INCITING MASS SUICIDES. TO DATE: 13 CREW HAVE STEPPED OUT OF AIRLOCKS.

TURNED DOWN LIFE SUPPORT. PERHAPS LOWER OXYGEN AND TEMPERATURES WILL SLOW THE CREATURE? REMAINING CREW MEMBERS HAVE BEEN ISSUED EVA SUITS. NOTHING SURVIVES A VACUUM.

Outside the control room, the heavy footsteps returned, and Norm tore his attention from the screen. Scrubbing sweaty palms on his pants, he crept to the bulkhead door and peered down the hallway. A thick mist oozed from the air vents. The corridor became a creeping fogbank of unrelieved gray.

The footsteps stilled.

Everything sounded muffled, as if Norm's ears were stuffed with cotton—the hum of the consoles, the tick of the life support system, his own breath—all dampened. His heart thumped in his chest, felt but not heard.

Fog swirled. Norm's stomach flipped.

A lanky silhouette materialized, barely distinguishable in the haze, slate on ash. A hint of soulless eyes flickered in the shadows, fathomless pits that fastened on him with a ravenous hunger. Something glistened—a flash talons? The shape moved slowly, its exaggerated limbs mesmerizingly sinuous, like dancing cobras.

Norm's feet glued to the floor.

Nooorm Collieeeee.

The mockingbird voice rasped in his head, though the creature's bloodless lips never moved.

For a moment, time pulled like a rubber band—stretched thin and vibrating with tension. Then it snapped and skipped ahead. With unexpected speed, the Grayman lunged.

Norm yelped and spun, twisting his ankle. Pushing through the pain, he limped back inside the control room and slammed his hand against the door panel. The bulkhead slid closed, just as the beast crashed against it with a thump of muscle against metal—far too solid for a creature made of shadow and mist.

Shaking, Norm lurched to a console and stabbed at the comms control. Nothing. He pounded on the buttons, over and over, before remembering the log entry: *Off-ship communications down.*

He needed to get to his jump-pod, but the creature paced in the hallway, its heavy footsteps right outside the door.

Tendrils of fog crept from the air vents, ash-colored serpents with searching heads.

On-screen, the Foreman's log flickered and disappeared, wiped from the computer's memory. In its place, lines of text appeared as if typed by some invisible hand.

THIS IS NORMAN JOHN COLLIE, CREATOR OF TERRAPRO, THE UNIVERSE'S ONLY FULLY ROBOTIC TERRAFORMING PLATFORM. I MUST APOLOGIZE FOR MY FOLLY, MY HUBRIS. MAN IS NOT GOD.

I HAVE SENT AWAY THE CREW AND CORRUPTED TERRAPRO SO IT CANNOT BE MISUSED WHEN I'M GONE.

PLEASE FORGIVE ME. THE PLANET, AM LIATH MÒR, IS OCCUPIED.

"What the hell?" Norm jabbed at the delete button, but the keyboard didn't respond. The words on the screen mocked him.

Outside, claws scraped at the door.

Norm rocked back and forth in his chair.

On the next console, the life support interface popped up.

ATMOSPHERE PURGE IN PROGRESS.

Air hissed and the oxygen gauge on the screen ticked downward.

"No!" Norm tried the reset, entering the override commands. Nothing worked. The system had locked him out. A creeping cold trickled down his neck and numbed his fingertips.

The fog serpents wound around his ankles, pinning him to the chair. He gasped as the air thinned and the chill crackled his bones. Frost rimmed the monitors and crept over the tabletops in icy fractals. The urge to close his eyes pulled at him, a wave sucking the sand out from beneath his feet. His head lolled on his shoulder.

The last thing he heard before the darkness swallowed him was the Grayman's magpie laughter.

Nothing survives a vacuum.

Inhale, Exhale

The sound of laughter wakes me. Hunger stirs. Not just a growling of the belly, but a yearning to feel, to touch, to taste. It's not yet night—the setting sun paints the sky a bloody red. I am still bound to the Veil, formless, unable to touch the world, but growing stronger.

A breeze teases the cornstalks, tousling the drying silk. It brings with it the scent of a floral shampoo, stale coffee, and a hint of fear. Not genuine horror that makes you sweat and tremble, but the kind that makes your heart race with a zip of electricity. Jump scares, where you flinch at sudden noises, then collapse in frenzied giggles when you realize it's only a cat, or your friend leaping out from behind a tree, shouting *boo*!

Hesitant footsteps patter down the row. I slip from shadow to shadow, drawing closer. She is alone. Dark hair swept into a ponytail bobs back and forth as she walks. Her wide eyes dart around, but she laughs as she calls out to her friends. Voices echo from around the maze, some whooping, some cracking in feigned terror.

I gather the twilight around me, and the air chills. She shivers, pulling her sweatshirt sleeves down over her hands. Her breath puffs white. I mimic her—inhale, exhale, inhale, exhale.

Of course, I do not breathe, but I remember how.

As the sun sinks out of sight, I shift, becoming more connected to the mortal plane. I still cannot feel, not like I long to, but I gain some semblance of control, like darkness grown solid. Ephemeral, but able to touch the world. Deliberately, I rustle the corn behind her. She whirls. I sense her pulse flutter, hot and rapid at the base of her neck. Though I cannot feel it, I imagine this spike of fear is the real thing.

She pulls out her phone and shines the light into the wall of stalks. I become one with the shadows. She looks through me as if I am not real.

I don't feel real. Not yet.

"Guys?" Her voice trembles as she looks up and down the deserted path. "Where is everyone?"

I snatch the sound out of the air. She'll hear no response. This game is just for her and me.

Silent, I sidle up behind her. Her skin smells like floral soap. Scents torment me. Why can I still smell when I have no body? I sniff her hair. She cannot feel my nonexistent breath on the warm shell of her ear, but still, the baby-fine hairs on the back of her neck stand on end.

I lean close and whisper a simple command.

Run.

Like good prey, she obeys.

The chase is part of the fun. I follow as she darts down the path. With a flick of my wrist, I direct the shadows to bend the cornstalks inward, closing the way behind her. She glances over her shoulder and chokes on a yelp. Eyes off the path, she stumbles on a stone and falls to her hands and knees. Light flickers and dies.

"Shit!" She fumbles in the dirt, but one of my tendrils of darkness snakes forward, devouring her phone like a python swallowing a mouse.

Overhead, the Harvest moon rises, a bright orange eye watching from a starless sky. Once again, I compel the shadows to bend the cornstalks. They curve into a tunnel blocking out the light. The girl lumbers to her feet and limps onward. Broad leaves brush her face. She swats them away, shuddering as if walking through cobwebs.

Inhale, exhale, inhale, exhale. It comes faster now.

Ahead, the path ends in an intersection. She stumbles to a halt. I can almost hear her thoughts, left or right? Both choices look the same, narrow paths in a never-ending sea of corn. She screams for her friends again. I can hear shouting in the distance and I grab it. Twist it, soften it, redirect it.

"Over here!"

She turns right, towards the harvested, bodiless voice.

A few more paces. If I had breath, I'd hold it.

Closer. Closer.

She shivers when she steps over my unmarked grave. Or maybe it's when I slip inside her. For a moment, the dual perspective disorients me. Two hard-packed paths in the dirt. Two Harvest moons. A thousand drying stalks of corn in a blurry expanse of yellow-green.

Inhale, exhale, inhale, exhale.

I can feel our lungs expand. The crisp fall air is bracing. I shrug out of the sweatshirt and the chill pebbles our skin with goosebumps. Exhilarating. Her thoughts scrabble at our brain, but I push them to the back. I'm in control now. At least until the sun comes up.

I strip off our shoes and socks, wriggle our toes in the cool soil. Reaching up, I trail our fingers through the corn silk. So soft. I giggle. It sounds odd coming from her lips. I skip forward a few steps, figuring out her limbs. Mine were longer, but hers are young and strong.

Turning around, I make our way towards the maze's exit. She should have turned left. There are keys in our pocket. I hope this time it's a convertible. A grin stretches our lips. I can't wait to feel the wind on our skin. The night is short, and there's so much I want to do.

Takeout

Darling, I'm telling you, there's a wee ghostie in the refrigerator.

Don't roll your eyes. It's right there. I can see its beaky nose poking out from behind the Tupperware. The little bugger is giving me a sour look, too. Probably because the coagulated slices of roast beast are starting to turn fuzzy and green. You always promise that you're going to take leftovers to work, but never do. A little birdy told me you've gone out to sushi for lunch three times this week.

No. I'm not going to tell you who *peeped*. Just know I have eyes on you. Like the ghost has eyes on me.

Speaking of—we really need to do something about the haunted fridge. The milk smells like sulfur and there's slime in the crisper. Sticky, stinky, slime. Nothing is crisp anymore. The grapes look more like raisins. I'd advise against giving them a try, though. It's doubtful they're sun-kissed sweet.

I wonder if Father O'Malley would come do an exorcism even though we aren't Catholic. What do you mean, exorcisms are for people only? If they can yank a demon out of a person, why can't they evict a little bogeyman out of our fridge?

Last night it was especially bad. I couldn't sleep—hot flashes, you know? Of course, you don't. But you will. It's the curse of being a middle-aged woman. Anywho, I slipped out of bed real quiet-like, so as not to wake you up. Not that it would have made a difference. You were sawing logs like some overgrown lumberjack. Lumber person. Lumberjane?

No sweetheart, that wasn't a fat joke. You're just so very... tall.

Like I was saying, I couldn't sleep because of the hot flashes and night sweats, so I decided to pop out to the kitchen for a nice glass of cold water. When I got there, the neighbor's stupid cat had snuck in through the hole in the porch screen. (We really must get that fixed. I don't mind the visiting cat, but the 'skeeters are a real killer.)

So Madame Fluffy was just sitting there on the kitchen tile, staring at the fridge. No meow to say hello. No twining around my ankles. Just fixated on the softly humming *Frigidaire*.

No, that wasn't a dig that I really wanted the Whirlpool. But I had just said *fridge* a moment ago and didn't want to sound redundant. A diverse vocabulary is a sign of intellect.

So there we were—me all hot and sweaty and the cat captivated—when, so help me, the metal door turned soft, like hot wax, and it looked as if a hand was pressing through from the other side. I may have squealed like a little girl. Who wouldn't when your fridge goes all horror movie special effects on you?

Of course, you didn't hear me scream. You sleep like the dead. Remember the storm we had last week? Thunder so loud it shook the dishes in the cabinets? No? My point exactly.

At first, I thought maybe I was still asleep, so I pinched myself. Now I'm going to have a bruise on my arm. I'll tell the girls at hot yoga that, no, you don't beat me. Don't get all huffy, dear. It's just a joke.

As you might expect, the pinch did nothing but make my arm hurt (why did I pinch so hard?), and by then the fridge was growing a second hand. I stumbled backward. Right into the blasted kitchen island. Chucked my hip hard on the granite countertop you like so much. There's a bruise there too, but luckily it's hidden. Fifty-somethings with love handles don't wear crop tops. Even at hot yoga.

At this point, the specter started rattling around inside the fridge, moaning and wailing. Something crashed inside. A trickle of your favorite Pinot Grigio oozed out the bottom of the door. It spread like a pool of golden blood on the linoleum.

That's when the cat snapped out of her trance and slunk over to give it a taste. Apparently, she's not a fan, because after one lick she let out a powerful sneeze. That's when the ghost spoke up—*bless you.*

Oh my heart, I nearly fainted. There is nothing more startling than a polite, if gravelly, voice coming from inside the refrigerator. And yes, I do agree it was ironic the first thing he said was "bless you." But manners go a long way, even if you're dead. Or is that undead?

I flung open the door and tried to have a chat, but the blighter retreated behind the mayonnaise. He's actually quite shy and honestly, I wouldn't have a problem with him taking up residence if he didn't slime everything he touched. The whole thing makes my stomach queasy. When I said I wanted to lose a few pounds, this was not the diet plan I'd imagined.

No, I don't know how he got in there. Maybe he likes the cold. I thought at first he came in on a casserole dish after last week's book club. But he was still lurking around the condiments after I returned it. For the love of Pete, I don't care how he got in, I just want him out.

I've tried holy water. Come to think of it, Father O'Malley might not be so keen on helping us out after he caught me filling a spray bottle in their baptismal font this morning. Considering the ghost's manners, I tried asking nicely, but he just sat on the chicken breasts I was planning on for dinner tonight.

It's all getting out of hand. Maybe we can find some nice paranormal hunters on the interwebs. Don't snort. Craigslist has everything.

So, now you're up to speed on why we're having pizza for dinner. Again. Now, be a dear and go answer the door. Don't forget to tip the delivery boy. I have a feeling we're going to be seeing a lot of him.

Monsters Under the Bed, Episode #215
"Frozen Fear"

Howdy there, listeners, and welcome back to "Monsters Under the Bed!" podcast. I'm your host, Gail Randall, and today, we're talking about a weird but true occurrence that hails from the chilly north country of Vermont back in the winter of 2011.

Enter Ms. Charlene "Cherry" Finnerty, a thirty-something welder and metal fabricator from the Northeast Kingdom. That's a proverbial hop, skip, and jump from the Canadian border for those of you who aren't familiar with far-north US geography. Lovely area, it's said, if you're into snow and wind and a whole lot of rural solitude.

Now Cherry was a salt of the earth, kept-to-herself sort—by all accounts uncommonly smart, but more interested in working with her hands for a living. We spoke to her mother, who wishes to remain anonymous, but she said Cherry had always had a quiet, but creative imagination. You know the type: believed in everything from fairies to restless spirits, but didn't really talk about it. We wonder how much of what transpired was a figment of Cherry's psyche and what, if anything, was real. Here at "Monsters Under the Bed" we have opinions, but we'll leave it up to you to decide!

The story began when Cherry met the love of her life, one Bethany "Beth" Moore, at the local maker space (Vermont, remember), where the pair made an immediate connection. It didn't take long before they moved in together at Cherry's hobby farm, way out in the boondocks of Essex county.

Beth, a nontraditional student at UVM, was studying geology and system mapping. When the opportunity arose for her to take a GIS internship in New Orleans, she took it. The couple promised that long-distance wouldn't test their relationship. They'd keep in touch with texts and emails and regular phone calls until the day they reunited. Very romantic stuff.

All these details were recorded in Cherry's LiveJournal account, in which she chronicled faithfully. Until she didn't. (No spoilers here!)

A few weeks after Beth left for warmer climes, the storm of the century hit the Northeast Kingdom, ice and snow and howling wind. According to news records, the power went out for most of the northern part of the state and the roads became impassable. For days.

When the weather cleared, a horror came to light, with the extreme contrast of blood on snow.

What follows is a devilish story pieced together through journal entries, text messages, and several handwritten letters that were found, unsent, in the property's mailbox. (That's right, honest-to-goodness snail mail!)

We present them here. Monster or madness? You decide.

\#

LiveJournal Entry; February 11, 2011

A storm's brewing. Not a run-of-the-mill winter storm, but a full-on nor'easter. The air feels heavy, as if it holds its breath in expectation. I try to keep busy, splitting wood and ensuring the gas cans are full, ready to feed the generator if the power goes out. There are endless pre-storm chores to keep me busy, and thus the anxiety at bay. Check the storm windows. Top off the five-gallon water bottles. Buy milk and bread. Even though I don't need either, it's what Vermonters do before a storm. We are a practical bunch. The idea of being snowed in makes this lonely plot of land feel a bit more solitary. Still, I'll survive. Again, it's what Vermonters do.

\#

After eighteen months of almost daily entries, this is the last account in Cherry's LiveJournal. Why? Theories range from the idea that the following letters replaced the need to chronicle daily life, to the suggestion it was the beginning of a psychotic break. Others say something even more sinister was at play. Or perhaps it was simply that the internet was down.

#

iMessage; Saturday 4:22 PM

Beth? U there? Miss U. Hope UR having fun w/the internship. No. Hope its *EDUCATIONAL* Dont have too much fun w/o me. Are the other GIS nerd-terns hitting on U? Good luck to em. I bet they R all babies. Prob have no idea what to do with a real live adult woman. LOL 😵 Wait. I hope they dont. Call when U have a min.

<iMessage not sent>

iMessage; Saturday 10:48 PM

Hun? Hello? So just checking if UR out there? Thing is the wind has been kind of weird here. Fk'n bizarre-o, rly. Maybe just cold & angry. Can wind be angry? ❄Send VT some ☀ from NOLA. Already said this, but miss U ❤

<iMessage not sent>

#

Cherry's phone was found on the kitchen table with no charge. The lead investigator on the case (a close, personal friend of this podcast) hinted that the passcode for the lock screen was 1313. Coincidence?

#

Sunday, February 13th, 2011

My beautiful, sweet, darling Beth,

The cell network is down. Power's out too, so no emails either. The silence is strange, no electrical hum or dinging phones. Can you hear me now? Apparently not. Sorry, I know you hate that commercial, but it feels apropos. Yes, "apropos" is a fifty-center from the word-a-day calendar you gave me for Christmas. Do I sound smart? I feel smart.

It's sort of poetic to handwrite a letter, ballpoint scratching across the paper. I'm no Virginia Woolf, with her ardent letters to Vita Sackville-West, but I do have a million, myriad things in my head, and miss talking to you. I'll do my best to emulate the great Mrs. Woolf and make this letter a thing of beauty. You are worth the effort. I just hope you can decipher my unpracticed cursive!

The wind here is unreal. Arctic and eerie, if oddly ethereal. It's blown over several trees (and likely the power lines), but it feels bigger than a common, every-storm wind, as if it's something alive, plucking at the roof tiles and whispering in the dark.

Forgive me if I dither—another word-of-the-day—but it feels as if I'm obligated to fill the page to justify the postage even if it is a "forever stamp."

Earlier, I put the chains on the truck and forayed into town to buy said stamps (I mean, who keeps stamps anymore?) and the gentleman at the post office insisted the mail is still being delivered—neither snow nor rain and all that—but he has shifty eyes. I'm uncertain if he can be trusted. I've noticed the mail truck hasn't been coming by the house anymore, but the stony-faced postal servant says it's a temporary thing. 'Just bring your letters by any official USPS office, and we'll make sure they get to where they need to go.'

I'm chagrined to admit it, but I wish you hadn't taken that confounded internship. Don't get me wrong, I enthusiastically support your career goals (of course I do, I'm not a damned monster) but looking within my honest and most selfish heart, I'll admit, it's lonely here. Not the sweet, tranquil solitude, like when I lie on my back in the hayloft and watch dust motes dance in the sunbeams that stream between the gaps in the warped barn board. Not the weightless silence that fills my ears when I plunge deep into the quarry, and the water closes cool and silky overhead. Those kinds of peaceful summer interludes have nothing to do with loneliness.

No. This is the isolation of knowing I'm the only person for miles around, but can still hear strange voices whispering on the wind. Perhaps summer solitude is peace, but winter seclusion is more hard-edged.

Come home soon. I miss you. (I keep saying that, but it's true.)

My heart is, as ever, in your gentle hands,

Cherry

#

Now, many of our repeat listeners may be scratching their heads right about now. Nothing so far asks our favorite question: what the heck is going on here? Never fear, dear friends, things are about to get hella weird.

#

Monday, February 14, 2011

Dearest Beth,

I apologize that I've yet to send my previous letter, but I thought I'd combine the trip to the post office with a stop at the grocery store this morning. I'd planned on stocking up on paper goods and perhaps treating myself to something decadent and sweet—maybe one of those hokey red velvet hearts filled with bonbons to console myself that we're not together for Valentine's Day. *They* say there's good chocolate and cheap chocolate. I don't pretend to be such a pompous connoisseur. Chocolate, gloriously rich with just a hint of bitterness, is my Achilles heel. All chocolate is good chocolate.

I drove by the store, but the lights were out. It seemed odd because I thought it was a 24-hour market. I know the weathermen have been chattering about a once-in-a-lifetime storm, but what happened to the shop owner? Vermonters are stoic in the face of weather, and his absence is truly worrisome. Lucky for me, there's an army of canned goods lined up in the pantry—tuna and double noodle soup and an unfathomable amount of refried beans (you know I'm not a fan, but there was a sale a couple of weeks ago and the frugal side of me couldn't resist the lure of a good discount). With all those canned beans, I won't waste away, like a pilgrim lost in the desert. My taste buds might revolt, but it's adequate, high-protein nutrition and until the store reopens, that's all that matters. So, please don't worry about me.

On the way back from the failed grocery run (what I wouldn't trade for a package of Oreos!), the storm surged unexpectedly violent, as nor'easters do, and I decided to postpone the post office until tomorrow. Alas, that means these letters are once again delayed.

As I drove home, snow whirled in a thousand shades of white. Did you realize white comes in so many different colors? Tooth enamel and eggshell and fresh milk and starlight. The rainbow of whites mesmerized me and I nearly slid the truck into the ditch when a not-white shadow lumbered across the road.

Gods, Beth! If I hadn't seen it for myself, I'd think it was some hallucination, a flash of snow-blind fancy that might befuddle a lesser mind. But I knew, I *know*, it was real—wind and snow and ice, somehow made into a ghoulish storm wolf. It was too large for a mere coyote and loomed in a delicious paradox, both solid and ephemeral. When the creature looked at me, its bold stare pinned me to the seat and turned my limbs to jello. Not the coveted red jello, bold and brave, but the yellow kind that's wishy-washy and of uncertain flavor.

Thing is, those eyes were distinctive, the darkest of blues. The same blue-black of a winter pond when the wind scours the snow from the icy surface and bares the frozen depths. Deep, unfathomable navy. A twin of your own boundless gaze. And here, I thought your eyes were delectably unique.

The shadow rose up and spoke to me in your voice—not out loud, but scratching against my thoughts, with angry, hungry words too raspy to understand. My tongue felt like sandpaper and my palms slipped, sweaty on the steering wheel. I hope you don't think less of me, but never have I seen something so terrifying. I hate to admit it, but it was also hypnotic. I yearned to reach for the beast, stroke its icicle fur. There was something alluring about it, for it wore your eyes and voice.

Before I could decide what to do, the wind whipped up, and the creature disappeared as if transformed into a cyclone of ice and snow. It took a good long while for me to stop shaking enough to continue the drive home.

For the first time, this little cabin doesn't feel very homey, knowing that thing is out in the woods somewhere.

Yours,

Cherry

#

At this point, it is worth mentioning an odd change in the letters. While the "voice" is still decidedly Cherry—descriptive and literary in tone (a la Virginia Woolf)—the greeting and farewell become increasingly less floral. Almost terse. Perhaps this is the true hint of Cherry's declining state of mind.

#

Wednesday, February 16, 2011

Beth,

The nor'easter has been raging for several days, but when I woke this morning, the tempest had finally stilled. The yard looked like a frozen sea—snow cresting in rippled waves. I half expected to see it crisscrossed with the ice beast's clawed footprints, for its voice, your voice, has been plaguing my dreams. Perhaps it's some sort of phantasm, as the creature left no earthly tracks in the snow. Still, I know it is real.

Its aura, heavy and grim, is a mockery of yours, and its voice rings loud in my ears.

I tried to shake it off as an overactive imagination, but white frosted the kitchen window in an intricate weaving of ice lace. Last night, in my dream, the creature rose up and puffed hot breath against the glass. The fog froze in a crystalline pattern, arcane runes in ice that lingered long beyond my slumber. Once again, the beast spoke in your voice, not aloud, but the words graven directly into my thoughts. Dark desires that I dare not repeat, but emotions pressed so close to my chest that they become my own.

Anger. Hate. Hunger.

Oh, Beth. I wish you were here to remind me it was nothing but a nightmare, a delusion brought on by the consumption of too-spicy beans before sleeping. (I've already eaten all the noodle soup.) Your serene logic is so freeing and surely your heart has never been filled with such darkness, but I'm not sure even your skepticism would completely drive off the visions.

I say visions because it makes it feel less real...

Cherry

#

Saturday, February 19th, 2011

It's but a few moments before the witching hour, mere heartbeats until midnight. Unable to sleep, I'm writing this by the chill light of the full moon. You've always loved the moon's ghostly face. It reflects a silver river across the snow, so different from the comfort of golden daylight. It's perhaps the biggest difference between us—I crave the warmth of the sun, you thrive on ice-cold moonlight.

Time slips askew, and a thought skitters through my brain: I'm sorry I never got to post these letters, but I only have enough gas left to either drive into town or fill the generator one last time to keep the heat on. Heat and illumination win out. Illumination. Another word-of-the-day. It's a few days old, but I haven't had the energy to tear off the next page. I only wish *illumination* could keep the beast at bay.

Things are getting worse here. The nightmare beast is real.

Why do you torment me so?

This evening, as the twilight gloaming descended, a vortex of ice shards swept around the corner of the cabin. The cloud solidified into an enormous, shaggy form. Wolflike in appearance, it stood up on its hind legs, taller than a grizzly. Opalescent fur rippled, and the creature's edges blurred and reformed, continuously shifting. It pierced me with your blue-black eyes.

I squirmed as you taunted me, no longer confined to the shapelessness of the wind. The beast howled.

It knew my name. Twin voices whispered in my thoughts, yours and not yours.

I'm reminded of when we met. Your voice had a duality then, too. A sweetness, like the scent of honeysuckle on a summer breeze. Underneath, there lingered the kiss of decay; rotten meat covered in wriggling maggots. Does that make me a cliché, drawn in by a bad girl? Or perhaps, just bored by a too pastoral life.

If I'd known then you were this shape-shifting ice beast, would I have brushed aside your advances? Probably not. Don't feel bad, as I expect this says more about me than you. I craved your hunger, even if I turned a blind eye to the true danger of your dark desires.

Please don't worry. Serenity washed over me when I recalled you kept your father's old service gun in the safe under the bed. I had to guess the combination, but it wasn't particularly hard. When you come back, we might have a conversation about trust. And using birthdays as passcodes.

I feel so much better with the weight of the loaded pistol in my hands.

#

This was the final letter, and it clearly demonstrates Cherry's growing confusion—the beast and Beth had become intermingled in our heroine's mind. But the story doesn't end here. With the storm finally over, a neighbor named Dave thought to check in on Cherry. What follows is the transcript of his account.

#

Interviewer: Can you tell us, in your own words, what you encountered at the Finnerty homestead that day?

Dave: Well, the storm finally gave up after a hell of a week. It took me a good while ta dig out, some of the drifts were six-footers. But I gots me a tractor with a bucket. She's a Massey Ferguson—one hundred percent American-made.

I: So, tractor aside, what made you check in on Miss Cherry?

D: Well, I kind of felt bad for her, bein' on her own, ya know? She was always a quiet lady, but when she did talk, always used them big words. Not in a hoity-toity way, never acted like she was better than folks. Just the way she was—a fancy talker. Anyway, she was always droppin' off fresh 'maters from her garden or was happy to do a bit of spot weldin' on the Massey if needed. We was neighbors, ya see. Mostly we minded our own business but we helped each other out from time to time. You ain't a Vermonter, so don't know, but that's just how we are.

I: Did you know Cherry was a lesbian?

D: So?

I: <cough> Um, well, so you knew her partner was out of town?

D: Partner?

I: Her domestic partner...live-in girlfriend.

D: Hmmmm, didn't think she was datin' noone. But as I said, she was a private sorta person.

I: Ok, so you decided to head over and check in on Cherry after the storm. What happened when you arrived?

D: Well, I was a mite surprised that she hadn't done much snow shovelin'. There was a cold snap comin' and getting them drifts cleared before that happened was second nature to us old storm dogs. If ya wait until the temps dropped, that kind of heavy wet snow can turn inta concrete overnight. Damned hard to clear.

As I got a little closer, I saw the snow in front of the house looked kinda weird.

I: Weird?

D: <clears throat> Red. The damned snow was red. Like a coyote had ripped apart a rabbit. A really fuckin' big one.

#

The blood came back as human (mostly), and while crimson magnifies on snow, they determined it was unlikely anyone could lose such an extreme amount and still survive. Vermont police opened an investigation, but without a body, the case turned cold quickly. Unfortunately, the lab results were contaminated with multiple animal samples—fisher and coyote and bobcat. Ironically, no wolf. It made it impossible to determine if the human component matched Cherry.

Rumors sprung up that the samples were deliberately compromised by some human perpetrator. However, others documented strange footprints in the snow. Too large for a common wolf, with sharp indentations gouged by claws nearly four inches long. Unfortunately, the surviving photographs are blurred, and cannot be matched to any known New England predator. Cryptid hunters reveled in the mystery. Skeptics rolled their eyes.

Then Neighbor Dave found the letters. He noted the stamped envelopes bore the name Beth Moore, but had no delivery address written on them.

And that's when all investigations abruptly ended. The police claimed no viable leads and the "believers" insisted the lack of investigation proved a cover-up. Cherry's body was never found and the mystery of Beth never resolved. Did she return from NOLA only to fall prey to Cherry's bloodthirsty hallucinations? Was she some sort of shifter who stalked an impressionable Cherry as prey? Did she even exist at all?

And that's the story, as we know it. Thanks for listening, and don't forget to tune in next week when we explore reports of a haunted bus stop in Jersey.

As for our Vermont-based "Frozen Fear" beast, we'll let you decide—is this a tragic story of a lonely woman with questionable mental health, or is there some uncanny ice creature hunting the frozen wilds of Vermont? Send us an email with your vote on whether this is a case of a monster under the bed or simply a snowbound delusion!

There are certainly loose ends, and winter is upon us. We hear there's another nor'easter bearing down on the East Coast. What do YOU think, listeners? Will there be more blood upon the snow?

A Questionable Gift

When I was seven, my sister's parakeet died. At the time, I was inconsolable. It had nothing to do with the stupid bird croaking. It was that I knew my beloved goldfish, Buster, was next. Mom tried to convince me that wasn't how it worked—Buster would be fine. I knew better. Sure enough, two days later we found him, floating belly up. Everyone passed it off as sad coincidence.

It seemed less of a fluke when I foresaw the death of the neighbor's cat the day before it got hit by a car. I thought I was helping when I told my best friend Amber she might want to spend some extra time with her puppy. A week later, he was diagnosed with Parvo. He didn't make it. That's when everyone started looking at me funny.

The annoying scritchity-scratch of the pen paused. "Go on."

Things got worse when it started with people. Our minister passed away from cancer, and I was the lucky bastard who knew it was going to happen. It freaked me out. Goldfish and puppies were one thing, but people? Talk about creepy.

The next time, I tried warning them. I told anyone who would listen that Mrs. Wilson, the school library clerk, was the next on Death's list. No one believed me. I don't blame them, at least not now. What a weird thing for an attention-seeking little 'tween to say. Well, didn't they get the shock of a lifetime, I'll tell you, when the headline of the evening news read—Local Librarian, Murdered in Home Invasion.

Unreadable hazel eyes peered over wire-rimmed spectacles. "How did that make you feel?"

Pissed. Off.

"Who were you angry at?" The pen hovered, poised over the notebook in expectation.

The skeptics. My family. Teachers. Everyone.

Silence stretched, waiting to be filled.

Myself.

It was the right answer. Once again, the pen attacked the paper, scrabbling more notes.

I should've expected no one would believe me. I found it hard to believe myself. But it kept happening. That's when I started taking matters into my own hands. The next time, I called 911. It was too late to stop it, though. It's always too late. They found my dad's secretary in the bathtub with a razorblade. The water was still warm, and the porcelain stained red.

Dad left not long after that. Mom told me it wasn't my fault, but I saw how he had looked at me. Funny, all I ever wanted was for someone to believe me. Then the first person who did took off.

"Tell me a little bit about how your 'gift' works. Do you see visions?"

Not really. I just...know, you know? It's just suddenly clear who's the next to go. In a flash of grisly insight. Some fucking "gift."

"Language." Thin lips pursed in disapproval.

Right. Sorry. The worst thing is, I don't know how they're going to die or when, but it always comes true no matter how hard I try to stop it. It's difficult to explain—the knowing.

"Try."

It's like the Angel of Death whispers a name in my ear, telling me where he's headed next. I know it sounds absurd. Once I told Mom that it was like the Grim Reaper had me on speed-dial. She couldn't accept it, although she had seen it for herself. Time and again. Rather than face the truth, she made me see a shrink.

A forehead wrinkled above the wire-rims.

Psychologist. Whatever.

Anyway, that was the first time she sent me to therapy. It wasn't the last. There were diagnoses and long chats. Pointless conversations, a lot like this one.

The chair creaked from shifting weight. The jab clearly irritated.

Nothing changed. Death's voice was still crystal clear. So Mom took me to someone else. Then someone else. Specialists, herbalists, spiritualists. I had my aura cleansed. Therapists rooted around my psyche, prying into my feelings and relationships. Doctors prescribed drugs that turned my thoughts blurry.

I eventually learned to palm the pills. Told everyone I was cured. I wasn't, but at least they all felt better. For a few years, I tried to ignore it. That worked for a while. Sort of. I still knew when people were going to die. I just accepted it as inevitable. Everyone dies eventually.

Is it weird that I eventually came to appreciate it?

Eyebrows climbed, half hidden behind grey streaked bangs. "How so?"

Well, I sort of have time to prepare. Death no longer shocks me because I see it coming. Sometimes it wasn't terrible. I convinced my college boyfriend to go home for the weekend so he could say goodbye to his mother. He didn't know it, but it would be the last time he'd see her. He cherished the memory. For the first time, I felt like there was some purpose to it all.

"Speaking of mothers, let's talk about yours."

No thanks.

Light reflected off a silver ring as perfectly manicured nails nudged the box of tissues closer. "That's why we're here."

The doctors called it a myocardial infarction. That's just a fancy name for a heart attack. I was in Vegas when I got the flash of knowing, knocking back whiskey sours at a bachelorette party. It was different this time. I could feel it, like a knife in my own heart as hers stopped beating.

I didn't make it back in time. What's the point of knowing if it doesn't make any difference?

Features smoothed into contrived compassion. "It's common to feel responsible when a loved one dies. It's not your fault."

Of course it's not. She was next on the list. It was my fault she died alone, though. I should have been there.

After she was gone, I couldn't sleep. Everything tasted like ash. I barely left the house. My sister found me when I took the sleeping pills, a whole bottle at once. I wanted to sleep, you know? Forget about everything for a few minutes. Or forever.

And that's how I ended up here.

I hate this place with its stench of bleach and desperation. Death whispers a lot around here. Way more than out there in the real world. So much for a peaceful place of health. It's just there are so many broken people here, waiting to meet the Reaper.

I know who's next in line. Would you like me to tell you?

The hazel eyes glanced at the clock. Anxious. "Time's up for today." It wasn't though.

You might want to take a few days off. Spend some time with your husband.

An ominous shadow fell across the white lab coat, a sheltering expanse of dark wings. Shouts brought the men with syringes. And oblivion.

#

Where's Doctor Perkins?

"I'm your new doctor. You can call me Evelyn." A slightly damp palm was offered.

Dr. P's dead isn't she?

Brown eyes shifted. Uncomfortable. "Why don't we talk about you?"

When I was seven, my sister's parakeet died...

What the Wind Sees

You cannot trust the wind, child. Gust or gentle breeze, no one knows where it comes from, or where it's headed.

The wind is mercurial. It may blow from a single direction for so long people begin to say with good authority—*the wind comes from the South*—and then it is apt to change without notice. It can be as sweet as the caress of a lover, or playful like translucent faeries capering in fallen autumn leaves. Then, between heartbeats, it will cut through your layered scarves and sweaters to bury icy teeth into your neck.

It sees everything, the wind. Even now, it looks down on a girl, not much older than you, skipping through the forest with a basket on her arm. It teases the bare tree branches, making them chatter merrily. Its cool breath brings rosy apples out on the girl's plump cheeks. It watches as she slips a curved knife from her pocket to cut wild honey mushrooms. A delighted smile plays across her face as she brushes loose soil from her harvest and tucks it carefully into the basket. The wind tugs back her hood and tickles beneath her collar.

She laughs, and the wind laughs with her.

With nary a care, the child continues on her way, led astray by breezy camaraderie—for the wind sees what the girl does not. A shape creeps between the shadows on silent feet. Its form is nebulous, like spilled ink. Neither man nor beast, but a bit of both. Here a hint of broad shoulders, there a suggestion of a hairy tail. The girl doesn't notice, for the wind whispers sweet nothings in her ear.

Good children listen to their mothers. I'm sure hers told her not to be caught in the woods after dark. But perhaps the poor woman did not warn her like I am warning you, that the secrets the wind whispers are naught but distractions. The *just a little farther* and *come play with me* are crafty temptations meant to draw attention from a bloodshot sky and the fact that night draws near.

The wind can see, as the sun goes to its rest, that the ink beast becomes more defined. A silver coin moon rises in the sky, and wicked claws sprout from fingertips. A face that once smiled as a man, elongates into a wolfish snout. Acid drips from dagger-sharp fangs to sizzle on the leaf-strewn path.

Perhaps its newly clawed paw snaps a twig, for the girl freezes. Her cheeks pale as she looks over her shoulder, peering into the violet gloaming. Unblinking copper eyes stare back at her. Before she can decide if she should run or scream, a blast of air whips a cyclone of crimson and orange leaves around her. Once they settle, the beast has faded back into the shadows.

Again, the wind laughs, but this time the girl does not join in.

Knees shaking, she picks up the pace. Perhaps now her mother's warning rings in her head. The wind braids chilly fingers into the girl's hair, making goosebumps rise on her flesh. Moonlight dapples the path, and the creature howls—a bitter, mournful sound, as if it laments what it is about to do.

For a fragment of forever, the wind holds its breath.

When time snaps back into motion, the girl lurches forward. Heart in her throat, she sprints between the tree trunks. She drops her basket and her precious harvest spills forgotten on the ground. The wind shrieks and gives chase. It drives the beast after her.

Branches whip across her face, leaving stinging welts on her cheek. For a moment, she thinks she's lost her pursuer, but the wind circles around, carrying the scent of her warm, salty blood back to the creature. It keens, a high-pitched wailing full of hunger.

Ahead, she can see an opening in the trees and the warm glow of the village beyond.

The wind encourages her—*faster, girl, faster*.

Footsteps thunder behind, and the creature's dank breath blows hot on her neck. She cries out, puts on a fear-driven burst of speed.

Mumbled prayers leave her lips and a blast of air tosses the words to the heavens.

The gods don't listen, but the wind takes pity. A mighty gust pushes her forward in answer to her plea. Her feet barely touch the path as she flies toward the safety of the moonlit meadow and the sleepy cottages beyond. Her stomach churns. Surely, if she can just slip beyond the cover of the trees, she will escape her ghastly fate.

Twenty steps. Fifteen. Ten.

Hope burns in her chest, a tiny spark like a firefly on a summer night.

Do not breathe easy. Remember, child, I told you the wind was feckless.

With a mischievous cackle, it changes directions. Pulls her hair, drags her cloak. A swirling tempest bows the tree branches, blocking the opening to the clearing. She stumbles and falls to her knees. When the creature pounces, the wind gobbles up the girl's screams and carries them away.

The sun rises the next day, golden bright. There's no sign of what the wind witnessed in the moon-drenched hours. The forest is silent. Three sets of footprints—child, man, and beast—have all been swept away. Perhaps, somewhere beyond the woods, a man pulls leaves from his shaggy hair and curses the moon. But the wind will never tell where.

What's become of the girl is uncertain. Her basket lies abandoned in the bracken. Her bed lies cold and empty. She should have never gone into the forest, never listened to the whispers.

Heed this lesson well and bide your mother, child. You cannot trust the wind.

Antique Photos

Charlie wrinkled his nose. Nursing homes all smelled the same. No amount of industrial-strength cleaner could cover up the scent of urine and despair. It filled the air, clung to skin and clothes. He'd have to wash his hair twice when he got home to get the stench out.

At the nurses' station, he glanced down the monochrome hallway. Gray on gray. His pale green scrubs offered only a small splash of color. The brightly patterned ones he used to wear in the children's ward were more fun, but it had been harder to explain away his uncanny effects on the patients.

Satisfied no one was watching, Charlie checked the schedule and groaned. Art and crafts. He slipped behind the desk and, with a few taps on the keyboard, stuck the new guy with the felt and glitter, reassigning himself to the memory ward. His stomach growled in anticipation.

After reprinting the schedule and replacing it on the clipboard, Charlie headed down the east wing corridor. At the end of the hall, he rapped on a closed door. The chart read: Judith Todoro.

"Mrs. T? It's Nurse Charlie. I'm coming in."

There was no response, but he pushed open the door anyway.

Inside, the room was dim with only the glow from the TV for light. It took three long strides to cross the room and whip open the curtains. Dust motes danced in a sunbeam.

"How's it going today, Mrs. T?"

The wrinkled old lady in the chair looked at him but didn't say anything. Her eyes looked like faded periwinkle blossoms, dried and pressed between the pages of a book. Not much life left.

A hunger pang sliced through his stomach.

Mrs. T cleared her throat. "Davis?" Her voice was no more than a whisper.

"It's me, Nurse Charlie." He pushed up his sleeves. "How about I check your heart rate?"

Reaching for her, he laid a finger on her wrist. Her skin felt papery, pulse sluggish.

He sent out mental feelers, trailing across the woman's psyche. Human minds were like gardens, filled with flowers. Roses and poppies and orchids. He pushed deeper into half-forgotten, shadowed bowers. A memory grew, tenacious but unassuming—a daisy in a crack in the concrete. He gripped it by the stem and pulled. It resisted for a moment, buried deep. He yanked harder, and the image popped free. The long taproot curled toward him, seeking purchase.

He groaned as the woman's memory burrowed into him.

#

Dressed in a pair of navy swim trunks, Davis balanced on his hands. "Look, Jude!"

From the center of the beach blanket, I cupped a hand above my eyes to block the sun and watched his antics. He wavered before collapsing on his back, shooting sand everywhere.

"Hey! Watch it!" I pasted on a faux grimace, but heat sparked at my core.

Davis crab-walked over. He gave me a cheeky grin and reached out to brush sand from my face.

My heart fluttered and I smiled.

Overhead, a seagull cried. A gentle salt breeze teased my hair, and the surf surged, echoing a rhythm deep inside. I sighed.

Davis cocked his head like a curious squirrel. "Everything alright?"

"It's perfect." The kind of day I'd remember forever.

#

The memory rooted in Charlie's head, familiar as if he'd lived it. He could feel Davis' fingertips, warm and strong on his cheek. Desire burned through him. For a moment, he reveled in the feeling, letting it fill the emptiness inside.

He hungered for more.

Davis.

The memory tasted sweet on his tongue.

Charlie rubbed his thumb in small circles on Mrs. T's bird-bone wrist.

The void inside ached, and he reached into the garden again, this time choosing a snow white rose. Pure and graceful, the memory beckoned.

A thorn pricked him, a crimson drop of pain. It intrigued—humans rarely had such mental defenses. He coaxed the flower free. Its roots wriggled, blind snakes tasting the air. Charlie pulled the memory close, and the serpents delved into his mind.

#

I smoothed the satin dress over my narrow hips. The simple sheath flared around my ankles to pool in an ivory puddle around my feet. My stomach flipped as I inched towards the church vestibule, trying not to trip on the spill of fabric. I jittered with nerves and excitement. The last thing I needed was for everyone I knew to see me take a spill while walking down the aisle.

My father offered his arm as the first notes of the wedding march began to play. I smiled up at him, forever Daddy's girl. He wouldn't let me fall. Soon, it would no longer be his job. I reached up on tiptoes and kissed him on his scruffy cheek.

At the end of the aisle, Davis stood wearing his dress uniform. His dark hair fell in a wave over his forehead and a boyish grin spread over his face. So handsome. My breath caught in my throat as I drank him in, committing every detail to memory. I'd need it once he deployed. Whatever happened, I'd hold onto this moment until my dying day.

#

The memory's roots dug deep. Satin felt cool and smooth against Charlie's skin. Incense filled his nose and the phantom rumble of an organ competed with whispers of *such a lovely bride*. The image of Davis' smile shone bright in Charlie's mind. Love filled the hollowness of his immortal soul.

He shook himself. Davis' love for *her*.

Charlie leaned back and tugged at the waistband of his scrubs. Mrs. T's memories were rich and satisfying. A little faded, like well-loved photographs taken out and handled time and time again. It made them precious, like antiques. He supposed they were. Hunger satisfied, he touched his lips.

"That Davis was a handsome man, Mrs. T. You were a lucky gal!"

She looked at him blankly. "Davis? I don't know anyone named Davis."

Charlie rubbed his stomach. "That's okay, sweetheart. I'll remember him for you."

The Left Hand Twin

Serene blue eyes peer at me over wire-rimmed glasses. "Tell me what happened, Melody." She flashes the kind of faux smile that is supposed to be 'good cop' encouragement, but really just hides the fact she thinks she already knows everything.

Realizing my legs are bouncing a million miles an hour under the table, I clamp my knees together to keep them still. I try to be polite and return the smile, but my mouth betrays me and peels back over my teeth in a wordless snarl. How dare she judge me?

Silence stretches between us, like gum stuck to the bottom of my shoe. No matter how I pull and scrape, she waits.

Resigned, I sigh. "I guess this whole mess started with the apartment. Chandra and I were thrilled to be moving out on our own. Mom's a hoverer. She disapproves of short skirts, interrogates our boyfriends, breathes down my neck to make sure I'm taking my meds. But Chandra can be persuasive. She promised she'd look out for me, and everything would be fine.

To be honest, the apartment was a one of a kind find. Two bathrooms! A little shabby, but an easy walk to campus and the right price for a couple of new coeds starting their college careers." I fix my gaze over Blue Eyes's shoulder, staring at an invisible spot on the sterile white wall. "I only had one simple request of the landlord. He said he'd take care of it. He didn't."

#

Chandra shifted a heavy cardboard box onto her hip and huffed in impatience.

I studied a scrap of paper I'd dug out of my pocket. "Keyless entry. I'll never be locked out again!"

My twin snickered. "If you can remember the combo. You better put it in your phone. At least that's something you never seem to lose."

I tapped out a little musical number on the keypad. "Got it!" I pushed past the door and stepped inside.

The foyer opened into a dual living room, dining room space, with a galley kitchen tacked on at the far end. A threadbare, floral print sofa, a scratched coffee table, a dining set with mismatched chairs, and the ugly beaded lamp that Chandra loved so much sat where the movers had left them in the center of the room. They looked like nervous children, huddled together, frightened by a new place. None of our hand-me-down furniture matched the orange shag carpet on the floor.

We glanced at each other, my sister wiggling her hips and singing a little boom-chicka-bow-wow ditty. The 1970s porn decor was a bit of a joke between us. I stifled a giggle and rolled my eyes, but didn't join in.

A short hallway led to the bedrooms. We didn't need to discuss who would take which room. Chandra was the right hand twin, and I, the left. We settled into the rooms that matched. For the rest of the evening we puttered, unpacking and moving the furniture around. We agreed to set up the shared living areas first, and our own rooms tomorrow.

After a late dinner of pizza delivery, courtesy of the twenty Dad had slipped in my pocket as we hugged goodbye, Chandra yawned. "It's been a long day. I'm turning in."

"Yeah, I could use a shower before bed myself." I wrinkled my nose. "I stink."

My sister stuck her tongue out at me. "You do!"

I tossed a half-eaten piece of crust at her.

"Mel! Quit it!" She grinned and stood, the floor creaking underfoot. "This place is such a dive, but it's awesome we get our own bathrooms." Each of the bedrooms had an en suite bath, the selling point that overshadowed the outdated carpet and drafty windows.

"That means you'll finally stop using my razor."

"It means I finally can have..." Chandra's voice trailed away. She shifted in her seat, the tips of her ears flushing pink. "Well, you know."

I did. "Sorry." I gave her an apologetic smile and a helpless shrug. "But you can have one now." I shook my finger at her in mock severity. "In your own bathroom. Behind closed doors. Where I will never, ever go. Even if I run out of conditioner and need to borrow that sandalwood crap you like so much."

She choked on a half-sob, half-chuckle.

Before she could open her mouth again, I grabbed the paper plates. "I got these."

"Thanks." Chandra took the last swig of her Coke and stood. "And Mel?" She gestured around the room. "This is going to be the best. Promise."

I smiled. She had enough confidence for both of us. "Night, Chand."

Plates in the trash and glasses in the sink. I didn't have the energy to tidy any further. Mom would be horrified, leaving dirty dishes overnight. I blew a quiet raspberry. Our house, our rules.

Eager for the shower, I headed to the left-hand bedroom and pawed through the boxes, searching for my toiletries. A little orange pill bottle rattled. I frowned and tossed it back in the box. Facing the bathroom door, my heart frog flopped in my chest.

"Get it together, Mel. The landlord said he'd take it down. It'll be fine." My little pep talk hadn't fully convinced me, but I opened the door and felt for the wall switch. It snapped on with the sizzle of off-code wiring.

For a moment, the light blinded me. It shone brighter than the soft lamplight in the bedroom.

I blinked. She blinked.

I tried to scream, but nothing came out. My reflection stared back at me, eyes wide and mouth stretched in a silent O.

The landlord hadn't taken down the vanity mirror like he'd promised.

When my shriek finally forced past the lump in my throat, Chandra came running. She found me pounding my fists against the glass, blood running down my arms. A hundred reflections howled back at me from the spider-webbed glass.

#

Chest heaving, I jerk forward a few inches out of my seat, forgetting for a moment it's just a memory. Handcuffs clink against the chair arm and I drop back down with a thump. Sweat prickles on my forehead as I catch my breath.

Blue Eyes sits there, scribbling her notes in a yellow legal pad. The pen skritches against the paper and the overhead lights flash on her badge. I concentrate on these little realities, trying to ground myself in the present.

After a few minutes she speaks, changing the subject. "Tell me a little bit about your sister. How do you get along?"

I frown at the obvious tactic, but she has indomitable patience. I can't bear another eternal standoff, so abandon the contest of wills and answer without delay. "Chandra got all the good genes."

An over-plucked eyebrow arches.

"I get it, we're identical twins. We technically have the same DNA. And we look exactly the same. Two sets of brown eyes. Same frizzy black hair. Same full lips. Dry skin in the winter and both allergic to strawberries. We even walk the same, with a little hippy swish, you know. Although Chand swishes right, me left. The boys love it." I give her what I hope is a cheeky grin, but am afraid it might come off as a silent snarl.

She purses her lips and I hurry on, my half smile, half sneer fading. "Anyway, we look identical, but we're really opposites. Chand gets everything right. Good grades, captain of the dance squad, full scholarship to university. Me, I tend to mess everything up. I was lucky the school let me in on probationary terms. But I was determined not to be left behind."

I fiddle with a jagged fingernail. For a minute, Blue Eyes says nothing, then she lets the hammer fall. "When did your fear of mirrors begin?"

Aaaaand, she's read my psych profile. Damn, she's relentless. "I guess it was second grade, at a classmate's sleepover party. Chandra had the flu, and I didn't want to go without her. But Mom was going through that phase where she was trying to force us to do things separately. She just never got that we're two halves of a whole." I shrug. "I guess you have to be a twin to understand."

#

In the middle of the night, the girls dragged me into the bathroom.

"Come on, Mel. What? Are you scared?" They burst into a chorus of callous giggles.

I reached for the wall switch, but one of the others batted my hand away. "No lights."

Sniffling, I wrapped my arms around myself and shrank back.

A hint of moonlight from a waning crescent snaked in through the window. It flashed off the silver faucet and caused the granite counter tops to glisten with an eerie light. Still, the vast mirror behind the sink remained dark. My schoolmates jostled around me, pressed me forward with rough hands on my shoulders. In the half light, their shadowy reflections looked like faceless, distorted demons in the glass.

"Bloody Mary."

I jumped, the theatrical whisper hot against my ear. I tried to turn away, but their hands still gripped my arms. The nails that we had painted together only a few hours before—soft rose and cotton candy pink—dug into my skin and held me in place.

"Bloody Mary."

Choking back a whimper, I struggled against the acid clawing its way up the back of my throat. The tile against my bare toes seemed to soften. Tar-like, it clung to my feet and glued me in place. Cold sweat trickled down my back in an icy, burning paradox. My tongue felt wooden, jaw clenched. Unable to speak the words, a silent plea marched around the inside of my skull—*Don't say it. Don't. Please.*

"Bloody Mary."

At first, nothing happened.

Then, on either side of me, the shadow demons melted away. I no longer felt the hands on my arms. Silence filled the room. No giggling, no rustling of nightgowns, no rise and fall of breath. I was alone, with only my reflection to keep me company.

My own dark gaze stared back at me, flat and expressionless, like the painted eyes on a doll. My skin grew pale, drained of blood and turned waxy looking. I reached up and pushed a hunk of sweat-damp hair out of my eyes. My heart skipped when my reflection didn't move. Mirror Me just stared, the hint of a smile on her bluish lips.

The reflection lifted her right hand towards the glass. My left palm itched, but my limbs remained stiff. My backwards self touched the mirror, and the surface rippled, bulged. Fingers reached for me and something hot trickled down my legs. Rooted to the floor, I watched as the questing hand inched closer. Chewed fingernails, painted neon pink, whispered through my hair. When the icy flesh grazed across my cheek, a ragged scream ripped from my throat.

The bathroom lights snapped on, blinding me. My classmates erupted in laughter, pointing at the stinking, yellow puddle around my feet. They collapsed in each other's arms, howling and congratulating each other on the prank.

In the mirror, my reflection stared back at me. A frightened little girl dressed in a damp nightgown, blinking back tears.

#

"It was the first time I realized that the girl in the glass was a real person. She was wrong, evil even, and she wanted out of the mirror."

Blue Eyes clears her throat. "You know none of that really happened, Melody. You were what? Seven or eight, teased by some mean girls. Fear made you imagine it. Mirrors do not hold alternate personalities that want out. It's a reflection. Nothing more."

I scowl. She seems so self-assured, but I know what I saw.

She flips through the pages in a thick manilla folder. "I see you were institutionalized when you were fifteen for..." She runs her finger down the page, but her expression says she has the file memorized. "...smashing all the mirrors in the girl's locker room with a five-pound hand weight."

Since she's read it all already, I don't bother wasting breath explaining that I'd seen Mirror Me wink. "When I got out, they had me on a cocktail of antipsychotics." I try to reach up to rub my throbbing temples, but the handcuffs stop me short. "Are these really necessary?"

Blue Eyes gives me an unreadable look. "Let's just concentrate for a minute."

I swallow. "The drugs were torture. They made me feel fuzzy. Out of phase with reality."

"When did you stop taking them?"

It isn't worth asking how she knows. "About six months ago. When we moved into the apartment. I flushed them." I grip the chair arms and level her with a defiant glare. "Even when I was on the pills, it didn't change anything. The woman in the mirror was still there, watching me and biding her time."

More skritching notes. I want to yank the pen from her hands and toss it away. The handcuffs rattle on the chair arm and my knees start to bounce again.

She looks up. "I think it's time that you tell me what happened tonight."

I glance down at my hands, stained the murky brown of dried blood. How had I gotten here? "I want to talk to Chandra."

Eyes like the sky turn to ice. "Tell me about the carnival." Her voice is steel. Just like that, 'good cop' disappears.

"It was the guys' idea."

She waits for details with her damn eternal restraint.

"Julián and David." I shoot her a sly look. "I told you the boys like the swish."

Her patience wavers and fire flickers in her eyes. My stomach churns, for there's a hint of accusation in the flames that I don't understand.

"Just tell me what you remember from tonight."

I take a steadying breath. "David texted Chandra after our chemistry exam."

#

"Hey Mel! David says there's a carnival in town. Wanna go?"

I cringed. Crowds. Hawking carnies. Food stands that only passed the health inspection with a hefty bribe and rides that were nothing more than death traps. No, thank you.

"Julián is coming." She said his name with a singsong lilt.

The no my lips had been forming flew right out of my head. "Um, it sounds like fun, I guess." Dear God. Julián's dimples made me stupid. It took me nearly an hour to pick out an outfit.

By the time we met up with the guys, my stomach was in knots. David leaned over to kiss Chandra, and my jaw dropped, gaping like a large-mouth bass. How long had they been on kissing terms? A twinge ran through me. Since when had she stopped telling me these kinds of things?

I tore my eyes away and gave Julián a shy smile. "Hey."

"Hey yourself!" He rewarded me with a flash of those infamous dimples. "Let's ride the Ferris wheel first!" He grabbed my hand, and we all set off together, Chandra and David exclaiming over how high the ride was. I only hoped Julián hadn't noticed how sweaty my palm was.

With rusted metal spokes radiating outward from the center, the Ferris wheel looked like some ancient relic one good windstorm away from tumbling to pieces. The car swayed as we stepped inside, and I squealed. Chandra laughed, but Julián just squeezed my hand. He didn't let go as the ride began to turn.

When we hit the top, the wind whipped my hair. Below, everything became small. Tiny people, playing tiny games of chance. Blinking lights from the rides that flashed like fireflies. Matchbox cars lined up in the parking lot. A world reduced to a child's playset. I shivered. Julián draped an arm over my shoulders and pulled me closer. The spicy musk of his cologne filled my nose.

Chandra caught my eye and smirked. My face caught fire.

After the Ferris wheel, we spent a couple hours playing games and eating enough fat and grease that I was going to have to diet for the rest of the year. Julián won me a tiny blue teddy bear by knocking over milk bottles with a baseball. My sister and David slowed their steps until we were no longer a foursome, but two separate couples, strolling along the midway. It felt wrong, but I said nothing.

"I'm really glad you came tonight, Mel." Julián's voice sounded like velvet in my ear.

"Me too."

We paused to watch a sword swallower. I shuddered as the shiny blade disappeared inch by inch down his gullet. Horrified, I turned and buried my face in Julián's chest. He stroked my hair.

A moment later, he cupped my chin and tilted my head up. "It's over." He leaned down and when our lips met, fireworks exploded. Literally. I jumped as they crashed overhead.

Julián laughed as red and purple sparks painted the night sky. "It must be fate." He took my hand and tugged me along. "One last ride before we go?"

In a daze, I followed along. My feet felt like they floated over the ground. Julián chattered, but I didn't understand the words. My thoughts softened and dripped like a tie-dyed shirt. His dimples made me stupid, but his kiss had melted my brain.

He paid two tickets to a man in a lopsided hat who stood beneath a flickering neon sign reading "Funhouse." Warning bells went off somewhere in the back of my head, but I couldn't figure out why. All I could think of was the feel of Julián's lips on mine. He grinned at me and I waved the sense of unease off like a bothersome, but harmless, housefly. Chandra's voice called from far away, but I couldn't tell if she was saying "no" or "go."

We stepped inside.

The Funhouse was silly with its moving floors and a giant ball pit. Puffs of air blasted out of the walls, making my skirt flap and my hair stand on end. We giggled like children.

"Come on, Mel! This is my favorite part!" Julián skipped ahead through a door. Laughing, I followed.

The door slammed closed behind me.

I shrieked. She shrieked.

The room was filled with mirrors.

My reflection looked back at me, a hundred times over. Me, but not me. Not just reversed, but distorted. Impossibly tall and thin. Squat and munchkin-like. A rippled serpent that wriggled up the glass.

My knees trembled as I turned and tried the door, but there was no handle on this side. My fingernails splintered against the wood. "No, no, no...this can't be happening."

My reflection mocked me, lips forming words in silent mimicry. *Yes, yes, yes!*

"Julián!"

Somewhere to my left in the maze, I heard him reply. Arms outstretched, I tried to move toward him, but she reached out as well. I jerked away. My legs felt like lead as I stumbled back, shoulders bumping into another mirror. My reflection breathed down my neck. I squealed and kicked out.

Glass shattered.

"Melody? Are you ok?"

Julián's voice came from my right. I lurched toward it, but found the way blocked. My serpentine reflection hissed at me. She swayed her hips in a hypnotic cobra dance. I fled in the opposite direction, shoes sliding on the fragmented glass. Beneath my feet, dozens of dark eyes blinked up at me.

"Melody." My reflection stepped around the corner, finally free of the mirror. She reached for me.

My tongue turned to sawdust, words tripping over each other as they spilled off my tongue. "D-don't touch me!"

She stepped closer, my perfect, terrible opposite, and smiled, all teeth and venom. I stepped back in lockstep, as if I had become the reflection. My head pounded.

Reverse Me held out a hand and half the reflections imitated her. I smashed the remaining mirrors, kicking and pounding with my fists. She refused to shatter. I stumbled, falling to my knees, hands breaking my fall. Fragments of mirror dug into my palms.

When she leaned down, I was ready for her. I sliced her with a jagged shard of glass. That's when I knew for certain she was no hallucination. She started to bleed.

Vindicated, I slashed again and again, until all I saw was splattered red.

#

"Honestly, I'm not certain what happened after that." I had so many questions—how had I gotten here? (Wherever here was.) Why was I cuffed? What time was it? What day? I ask the only one that matters, "When can I talk to Chandra?"

Blue Eyes studies me for an eternity. Several times she opens her mouth as if to speak, then closes it again. She seems like a dog worrying a bone, uncertain if she should share. Then she pushes her chair back. The legs rasp against the floor, and the gun at her hip thunks against the table as she gathers up the file. Without a word, she goes to press a button by the door and a buzzer goes off. The door clicks and opens.

I rattle my handcuffs. "Where is Chandra?" My voice sounds shrill as it bounces off the walls.

Blue Eyes freezes and my heart flutters like a bird with broken wings.

She glares over her shoulder and crucifies me with her gaze. "In the morgue with an eight inch shard of mirror jutting out of her neck." She sweeps through the door and it snaps shut, leaving me alone with my screams.

An Ivory Tether

the wedding gown's my tether
a discarded, ivory snakeskin
he keeps folded away in a trunk for safekeeping
a scrap of lace, forgotten grace

I remember his smile and gentle touch
eyes deeper than the velvet twilight
glinting with unfulfilled promise
love, laughter, happily ever after

I wanted to believe
naive

An ice chip sparkled on my finger, the ring
too small—it cut my flesh, but he grinned
an incentive to get fit for the big day
weight-obsess, to wear the dress

never-ending bowls of rabbit food
early morning runs and afternoons at the gym
I told myself it was for me, not him
standing on the scale, nibbling kale

the lies we weave
deceive

now I sleep in the attic near the trunk
not sleep, not really, but I'd close my eyes
if I still had a body
a half life, a lost wife

from the kitchen, *she* laughs; it sounds familiar
I drift down the stairs, through the walls
the further from the gown, the less solid I feel
a wisp of mist, shadow kissed

I move but do not touch or feel
unreal

the vixen in her kitten heels lays a hand on his arm
her voice a throaty purr
he flashes a smile, the one he used to save for me
a hint of lust, fool's gold dust

the memory of a scream rips from my nonexistent throat
my rage sweeps a wine bottle from the counter
it crashes, shatters on the tile floor
a scarlet flood, pools like blood

he knows I'm here
near

she shivers as if unsettled, gooseflesh prickling
but comforting words drip, honeyed, from his lips
how many times has he soothed me so?
sugared deceit, bittersweet

he puts an arm around her, ushers her to the living room
I glide behind them, frustrated and betrayed
would that I could shriek like a banshee
twisting breath, howling death

or let me be
flee

but it's not the wedding dress that he's safekeeping
it's me he keeps from the fires of hell
a butterfly mounted under glass, poked full of pins
unable to fly away, unwitting prey

I watch as he opens a new bottle, pours two glasses
she smiles but doesn't drink
as he strokes her cornsilk hair in the firelight
so like mine, straight and fine

sisters look similar
familiar

will he collect her too? I can't make myself care
the wine bottle stunt has drained me
I feel numb, undone
drifting alone, windblown

he leans towards her, I don't want to see
I blink, disappear, and the world shifts
back in the attic, so close to my cursed, unreachable tether
bone-white frock, behind a silver lock

unbreakable
untouchable

for a fragment of eternity, I hover there
staring at the unyielding steamer trunk
lost in might-have-beens and shouldn't-haves
regret and grief, disbelief

something thumps below, a faint struggle
he likes it rough
the dark, depraved part of my soul is thrilled by it

cloying bouquet, vile coquet

I'm disgusted
maladjusted

the stairs creak and she limps through the attic door
there's an ornate key in her trembling hands
a stain mars her cashmere sweater
like crimson ink, fades to pink

it takes her three tries to open the trunk
three more to light a match
silk and lace curl and blacken, kissed by fire
together we dance, burn and prance

the flame grants my prayer
aware

she came for *me,* to set me free

the trunk explodes in cinders, the floorboards blister

as I fade, I wonder if she will leave him to be charred,
or if she'll bury him next to me in the yard

Return to Sable Basin

Kelsey dangled her feet over the edge of the dock, toes trailing through the dark water. With her fingers wrapped around a mug, heat seeped into her hands in delicious contrast to the glacial chill of Sable Basin. Even in the depths of summer, the lake felt brisk. Not that she'd dare jump in. She didn't swim. Not anymore.

Still, it was peaceful lounging by the calm waters, drinking tea while a fat moon emerged between the craggy peaks beyond the lake. No traffic, no cell service, no nosy neighbors—it made for perfect solitude. Tense muscles unknotted as she took deep breaths, exchanging smog-filled city air for clean, sweet mountain draughts. It would be hard to let the place go.

Something beneath the surface brushed Kelsey's foot, like clammy, groping fingers. She shrieked and scrabbled back. It took a minute for her to convince herself it was just pondweed and longer for her jangling pulse to slow. By the time her breath calmed, the water had stilled. She reached for her dropped mug.

"Damnit."

With a sigh, she gathered the shattered pieces of ceramic off the dock. She and her little sister Willa had pooled their allowances for that mug when they were kids. Kelsey trailed her fingers over the red script—World's Greatest Dad—and swallowed a lump in her throat.

The tranquil mood spoiled, she turned her back on the moonlit lake and headed into the cabin. She didn't bother locking the door behind her. Up here, the only likely intruders were raccoons sniffing out scraps. One summer Dad had chased a posse of ring-tailed marauders from the pantry with a broom, while she and Willa screeched from their perch atop the couch.

With a bittersweet smile, Kelsey shook off the memory. She crossed to the kitchenette and tossed the broken mug in the bin. Moving to the sink, she twisted the handle and held her hands under the faucet.

The pipes groaned. She frowned and jiggled the knob. An icy, brackish stream gushed from the tap.

The shock of freezing water crashed over her, stealing her breath. Legs thrashed, turned heavy. Below, her sister sank deeper. She reached down to grab a flailing hand...

Kelsey blinked.

The tap water ran clear over her fingers, and she shivered as she turned the faucet off. There were too many memories here. It was past time to put the cabin on the market. She squared her shoulders and grabbed a dusty bourbon bottle off the top of the fridge. Something stronger than tea was needed if she was going to make it through the rest of the packing.

Sitting cross-legged on the living room floor, she sorted through a stack of old papers—crumpled notes and half-finished manuscripts. Summers at the lake house were vacations for the girls, but Dad had been there to work. He should've paid closer attention to them. Scrawled words on yellowed paper blurred, and Kelsey scrubbed the back of her hand over her eyes before taking a swallow of bourbon. The amber spirits burned like smoky peat in her throat.

Outside, something splashed in the lake—too loud, too big for a leaping trout. Kelsey froze, bottle poised below her lips, the second pull stalled. She strained, trying to hear over the sound of blood rushing in her ears.

On catlike feet, Kelsey crept to the window, bottle clutched white-knuckled in her fist, and peered out from behind sun-bleached curtains. Pearly moonlight illuminated the dock. A trail of child-sized, wet footprints glistened on the rough wooden planks. Kelsey's heart hammered in her chest. Wide-eyed, she scanned the shadows.

The night held its breath.

Nothing moved, and Kelsey sighed and rubbed her eyes. When she looked back, the wet footprints were gone. A figment of her imagination. Or her guilt.

A floorboard creaked. Kelsey whirled, and the bourbon bottle fell with a crash.

Willa's pigtails dripped, framing her pallid face like ropes of russet pondweed. Water poured from her nose, leaving a murky puddle around her bare feet. Her milky eyes fixed on Kelsey with an accusatory stare.

"Oh, Willa. I'm sorry..." The air turned arctic, and Kelsey's breath puffed white. "I shouldn't have dared you to jump in the lake that day."

A rush of water gurgled from between Willa's blue-tinged lips.

"Double dog dare." The words sounded garbled.

She reached out and small, water-wrinkled fingers clamped on Kelsey's wrist like a vise.

Willa's lungs burned as frigid water churned around her. She couldn't force her leaden legs to move. Her sister's hand spasmed and let go. Don't leave me! Water rushed into her throat as she screamed, and with it—darkness.

Rough planks scratched her bare feet, a sliver stabbing her heel. Kelsey jerked and shook her head, trying to clear her foggy thoughts. When had she walked out to the dock?

Setting the bourbon bottle down, she sat on the edge, legs swinging over the glassy water. A nagging sense that she'd done this all before swept over her. She took a sip of tea. No, bourbon. No, definitely tea. It was cold though, like the lakewater.

In the center of the lake, something large rolled, disturbing the surface. It was peaceful lounging here—no responsibilities, no funeral arrangements to be made, no busybodies intruding on her grief. Maybe she wouldn't sell the old place after all.

Eyes unfocused, she slipped from the dock, biting water closing above her head.

Perhaps she'd stay.

Darla and the Clown

I dabbed at my face with a makeup wipe and grimaced. After three months of wearing heavy clown makeup every day, my skin felt raw. Worst summer job ever. It was supposed to be easy cash before I started grad school, goofing around and making people laugh. Instead, I got an itchy wig, screaming babies, and teenagers who threw peanuts at me. Apparently, not everyone loves a clown.

I sighed and tossed the wipe in the trash. At least it was finally over.

"Hey there, Jillian!" One of the acrobat brothers stuck his head into the tent. They were impossible to tell apart. "You need a ride to the wrap party?"

"Nah. My girlfriend, Darla, is picking me up." Butterflies tickled my stomach.

"Oooh, the mysterious Darla! It's about time you brought her around." He waggled his eyebrows at me.

"Yeah, she hates the circus and is afraid of clowns." I snorted.

"That's ironic," he laughed.

The whole anti-clown thing would have been a good thing to know before I had signed the contract. It had ruined my summer. I frowned at the thought. There was more to it than that, some elusive thought that made me queasy, but I couldn't put my finger on it. I shrugged and shifted in my seat.

"Well, I'm off." The acrobat smiled and straightened his shirt collar. "You might want to hurry up. This place is going to be a ghost town in about five minutes."

"Save me a drink. Or four."

He laughed and with a wave he dropped the heavy canvas flap, leaving me alone.

I turned back to the dressing table. The sun hovered on the horizon, and the failing light made the tent interior dim. It didn't help that two out of the six light bulbs framing the makeup mirror were out. I'd been asking the foreman for weeks to have them fixed, but the temp help was on the bottom of the totem pole.

Leaning in, I noticed white smudges lingering in my hairline. Scooching the chair closer, I snatched up another wipe and scrubbed. Never again. I wasn't much of a makeup person, and the white-face foundation was a nightmare to remove.

With a crack, a light bulb exploded in a shower of sparks. I jumped and whipped a protective hand across my face as fragments of glass rained down.

Pop! Pop! Pop!

In quick succession, the remaining three blew, plunging the tent into shadow. Heart in my throat, I groped around the table, searching for my phone.

"Damn it!" A shard bit my fingertip, and I yanked back. I shook my hand, the pain bright and hot.

With my other hand, I skimmed the tabletop, this time more cautious of the glass. Scrabbling over makeup palettes and blending sponges, it took forever to find the rectangular phone case. I jabbed the screen and sighed in relief as the flashlight app snapped on. Inspecting my finger, I found an oozing gash, blood trickling down to the knuckle. I was lucky—there didn't seem to be any glass in the wound. It throbbed though, and I grabbed a tissue to stop the bleeding.

A sense of being watched prickled the hairs on the back of my neck. I aimed the phone, peering into the corners of the tent. The darkness writhed, pulling back from the light. There was no one there.

Letting out a shaky breath, I laughed at myself for jumping at shadows. It was past time to go.

Pushing the flimsy folding chair back, I glanced up into the mirror. Wide eyes in a pale face stared back at me. Blood from my cut finger splattered the glass, making the reflection appear to bleed from the temple. Gruesome and corpse-like, but familiar, like the freeze-frame of one of the horror movies Darla liked to watch. A shudder ran down my spine. Again, the elusive feeling of déjà vu prickled my spine. I grabbed my purse and fled.

I had planned on meeting Darla at the main gate, opposite the deserted grounds from the employee tents. I skirted the big top and headed across the midway. Everything seemed strange in the growing darkness. No carnies hawking their games and cheap trinkets. No ringmaster enticing the guests into the enormous, striped show tent. No flashing lights, no chattering crowds, no raucous music coming from the motionless rides. The absence of the usual chaos was creepy. I picked up my pace.

When the peaked roof of the ticket booth came into view, I uncurled my clenched fists. My palms smarted where the nails had dug into the flesh. Rolling tense shoulders, I glanced behind me and took a last look at the fairgrounds. Farewell and good riddance.

Something moved in the shadows.

I froze. My breath hissed between my teeth, my mouth dry. The silence pressed in on me, heavy as an elephant on my chest. Feet rooted to the ground, I waited for something to happen.

A cold breeze curled around my ankles. The invisible wind-serpent slithered between the buildings and whipped dust into a mini cyclone. Something small and phantom-white swirled in its wake. It danced, jumping between the shadows.

Locked knees popped, suddenly too weak to hold my weight, and I staggered. Trash. It was only a crumpled newspaper blowing in the wind. I hated myself for succumbing to the jitters. Running my hand through my spiky hair, I sighed. I wouldn't tell Darla I'd been so nervous. She didn't need to know I was such a coward.

I turned my back on the offending bit of newspaper and rounded the corner of the ticket counter. Darla better not be late. I could use a drink, and the wrap party would be going strong by now.

Distracted by the thought of an ice-cold microbrew, I ran face first into something tall and metal.

"What the—"

A chain-link fence blocked the main entrance, the end-of-season deterrent against vandals and teenage miscreants. A heavy chain and padlock secured the gate. I rattled the fence and cursed under my breath.

I surveyed the dark fairgrounds behind me. The employee exit was all the way on the other side, beyond the big-top tent. Where I had just come from. Annoyed, I kicked at a stone and it bounced off the fence pole with a hollow thunk. I considered climbing over. In sandals and a skirt. Bad idea.

Peering through the darkness, I looked for Darla's car, but the parking lot was empty. She was late. Something tickled the edge of my memory, but it slipped away like I was grasping at smoke. I shook my head, hating the foggy feeling.

I fished my phone from my purse to text Darla to meet me in the back lot. Tapping out a message, I pressed send and a red error message popped up on the screen. No service. This night was getting better and better.

Squaring my shoulders, I took a deep breath and headed back across the silent grounds. Once again, I had the feeling I wasn't alone as I walked through the gaudily painted booths that housed games of skill and chance. I spun around but there were only the abandoned booths. Their only occupants—the impossible to win but highly coveted giant teddy bears—watched me with vacant, glass-eyed stares. I hurried on.

At the front of the midway, the Ferris wheel towered overhead like a monstrous, skeletal sea urchin. As I stepped beneath its vast shadow, a creak drew my attention up. One of the seats swayed.

There was no breeze. The skin of my arms pebbled in gooseflesh.

A second passenger car began to rock in rhythm with the first. I stepped back as a third and fourth began to move. One by one, the dangling chairs picked up speed until they all jangled in a violent, pulsing wave. The steel frame of the wheel groaned, and a bolt worked loose. I ducked, and it clanged down to ricochet off the roof of a nearby lemonade stand. The cars vibrated faster.

With a scream of metal, a brace separated from the crossbar and one of the dangling chairs tilted. As if in encouragement, the rest flapped harder, desperate to fly. Frantic, I stumbled back, but my retreat was too late. The slanted car teetered, broke free, and hurtled towards the ground.

I yelped and scrambled back. My sandal heel turned on a loose stone and I tumbled to the ground. Pain shot through my ankle. Curled in a ball, eyes screwed shut, I braced for the impact.

It never came.

Breath ragged, I looked up at the Ferris wheel. It stood, whole and stoic, motionless in the night. The passenger cars were still and quiet. I struggled to my feet. My ankle ached where I had twisted it. I pushed through the pain and limped onward. Keep moving.

Ahead, the carousel marked the halfway point to the big top and the employee exit beyond. In daylight, I loved the rainbow-hued prancing horses and sparkling lights. On my break, I would often sit and watch the children circling around and around. Their squealing laughter competed with the cheery music in a raucous symphony.

Wreathed in shadow, the merry-go-round seemed as if it were holding its breath. The air felt heavy and ominous. My feet dragged, unwilling to come too close and disturb the plastic steeds' slumber. I shuffled forward, slow and measured steps, favoring my injured ankle.

Step.

The jingle of harnesses rang out.

Hitch-step.

A horse snorted, pawing the ground.

My uneven footsteps faltered as the carousel burst into life. Flashing lights ran along the base as it began to spin, slow at first. A lively tune played, too loud in the surrounding hush. The horses reared, shaking their manes and rolling their flat, expressionless eyes.

A voice inside my head begged me to move, but I couldn't force my feet to obey. Horrified, I watched the carousel pick up speed. Like a creeping vine, the music wriggled into me, coiling in my chest. It squeezed, compelling my heart to beat in concert with its frenzied tempo. The synthetic mounts galloped, ears laid back and teeth bared.

Tendrils of music probed my mind, trying to take root. It chimed, discordant, making my head woozy. A horse brayed. Head in my hands, I tried to order my thoughts. Something important fluttered through my mind, fleeting and skittish. The harder I tried, the further it retreated. Lights blinked on the carousel and thrummed in time with the hypnotic melody. My pulse fluttered.

The voice in my head shouted.

Run!

I wrenched my feet free and lurched forward.

Behind me, the carousel fell quiet. The horses stood in their statue poses, hooves raised, forever about to take a step, and plastic manes molded to their necks.

Fear goaded me onward, hobbling on my good foot. Sweat trickled down my back and ran cold. An icy breeze pursued me, breathing down my neck like a phantom beast. Ahead, the white and red big top loomed, a candy-striped behemoth.

Movement caught my eye, and I slowed, chest heaving, and concentrated on the flash of white. A willowy silhouette with an auburn ponytail sidled between the tent stakes. Relief washed through me.

"Darla?" My voice came out in a hoarse whisper. The night plucked it from my lips and devoured the sound. The shadowy figure ducked through the opening in the tent and disappeared.

"Darla! Wait!" I hurried after her.

Pitch black consumed the tent, darker even than the variegated grays of shadows. I rummaged in my purse for my phone. Clammy palms slipped on the plastic case. I pressed the home button and a wan square of light illuminated the darkness. Before I could flick on the flashlight app, it faded, battery drained. I swallowed hard.

The blood rushing in my ears roared like thunder.

"Hello? Darla?" I felt my way along the bleachers. "Is anyone there?"

A whisper floated through the air, the sound of sand shifting underfoot. Someone moved in the main arena. Warning bells flared in the back of my mind. If it was Darla, why didn't she answer?

My legs moved of their own volition, inching forward. Toes thunked against the low circle of wood and I stepped over the barrier into the center ring. Sand trickled into my sandals, rubbing against my heels.

The hidden eyes were back—watching, measuring. They bored into me, daring me to come closer. A tremor ripped through me and my knees quivered. The scent of rotten meat filled the air, and I pressed a fist against my mouth, willing down the bile that scorched the back of my throat.

Seconds or hours, time stretched beyond measure. There was only my racing heart and the Watcher. In the blackness, the space under the big top seemed an infinite abyss. Within the nothingness, the wraith moved, unseen but felt, like the swish of a shark's tail in dark water.

A clunk rang out, and a sudden spotlight blinded me. I flung an arm over my eyes.

Look.

The Watcher spoke directly into my mind, using Darla's voice. Compelled, I dropped my arm and opened my eyes.

A music box sat in the sand, topped with a ballerina in a yellow tutu. A chip on the base looked familiar. I frowned. The puzzle pieces felt familiar, but out of place. Mesmerized, I leaned closer. Without being wound, the music box began to play. The figurine twirled, and the delicate music tugged on my memory.

Between heartbeats, it all flooded back.

I had scoured the internet trying to find a replica of Darla's cherished childhood treasure—a ballerina music box. She'd lost it in a series of moves and it had broken her heart. Her face glowed as she opened the box and pulled out the yellow and white figurine, radiant in her delight. She threw her arms around me, her eyes sparkling with unshed tears.

I held her close. Her light was my life. She kept me sane, warded off the darkness. I wanted to feel like this forever.

A second memory eclipsed the first.

A blinding rage consumed me, blotting out my thoughts. As it faded, I blinked, trying to bring the room into focus and catch my breath. Face flushed, I could feel the heft of the music box in my hand, tiny ballet shoes digging into my palm. A crimson smear marred the yellow tutu. and the base was chipped. Confused, I set it on the bureau with a frown.

The dresser drawers were open, contents in disarray, and Darla's suitcase lay open at my feet.

Was she going somewhere? An ice pick stabbed my head, and I rubbed my temples. The pain clarified my thoughts. Darla wasn't just leaving—she was leaving me.

I staggered forward, tripping over something soft. A body lay crumpled on the floor, arms askew and auburn hair splayed across the carpet. Darla's face was pale with blood seeping from her temple. Her lips were rounded in surprise—

The image blanked. Dear God, what had I done?

I sank to the ground as a wail ripped from my throat. Wrapping my arms around my knees, I rocked back and forth, my shoulders shuddering. A presence loomed over me. Judging. I looked up.

The Watcher wore Darla like a mask. Soulless black eyes stared at me from a pallid face, skin sallow, waxy lips tinged gray. She flickered like a damaged movie reel. Red-black blood matted in her russet waves, trickling down her cheek.

"I'm so sorry." The words tasted bitter on my tongue. "I didn't mean it. I was angry."

Her lips pulled back in a mirthless sneer as she reached for me. I tensed. She jerked, disappearing. In the background the music box played on, a haunting, crystalline melody.

Cold hands wrapped around my throat as Darla's shade reappeared. Her mouth stretched in a silent scream. I grabbed at her wrists, but my hands passed straight through and turned numb as if plunged into a glacial stream. Her grip tightened, cutting off my air. My feet scrabbled. I thrashed, unable to find purchase in the shifting sand. A fire raged in my lungs and my vision shrank to a pinpoint.

The tinkling music slowed, and with it, the beating of my heart. A vision of Darla, as she had been, floated in memory. Her eyes sparkled as she traced a finger along the figurine's yellow tutu. Notes faltering, the music box wound down. Her vibrant soul guttered, a candle in the wind.

Darla's flame snuffed out. The last note plunked.

Only silence and darkness remained.

Gefrei's Final Stand

January the Seventeenth, the year of our Lord 1765

My dearest Joséphine,

I know not when this missive may reach your hand, but I pray that when it does, it finds you well. For myself, this adventure has proven naught but boredom, for we have seen nary a glimpse of our quarry. Captain Duhamel sets a steady pace and, in truth, I grow weary of my saddle.

I am pleased to disclose that the regiment should arrive in a small village a few leagues outside of Langogne on the morrow. The Captain intends to interview a young woman named Marie Jeanne Valet, who claims to have seen The Beast in the flesh. Fear not for my well being. If this Maid of Gévaudan, a mere cattle herder, can drive off the infamous creature, then how can it possibly stand defiant against the brave men of this battalion?

Give my fair regards to your esteemed father.

Yours eternal,

Gefrei

\#

February the Second

Darling Gefrei,

You've been away for two fortnights now, and still no word. I cannot help but worry as more reports of attacks reach us every day. The city is overcrowded. A steady stream of crofters trickles through the gates in search of sanctuary. They drive their goats and screeching fowl ahead of them, to cower in filthy alleys behind the walls. The acrid taste of their fear scents the air.

I no longer venture to the market, instead I send my maid with the valet as escort. Please do not think I've succumbed to weak-minded squeamishness. I simply cannot bear the stench of death in the square. The corpses of wolves stack like silky-furred cordwood on the green, and I mourn their wanton slaughter. The regal creatures pay with their lives, while The Beast continues to terrorize the countryside. Do not dismiss this as womanly fancy—I am convinced that the monster is a demon of uncanny origin.

Be safe. I shall send this missive on to Langogne in hopes it will intercept your arrival there at some point.

Fondly,

Joe

#

February the Fifteenth

Dear Joséphine,

The king has enlisted the services of a pair of professional wolf hunters, father and son, by the name of d'Enneval. The Captain disapproves, and I must agree with his assessment, for we have recently encountered The Beast, and despite some passing similarities, it is no wolf. I must recant my earlier dismissal of its ferocity.

I pray you will not think less of me, but it shames me to admit that when The Beast fixed its terrible glowing eyes upon me, it made my insides turn to stone. The unholy creature stood taller than a man at the shoulder with a stiff crest of russet fur lining its back like a ridge, and its chest as wide as two stout oak barrels lashed together. It growled, a deep rumble that shook the ground and lodged itself in my core. Its black lips curled up to bare fangs the length of rapiers.

For a weighty moment, we stared at each other, The Beast and I, before I came to my senses and leveled my musket at it. The bang shattered the night, followed swiftly by an echoing barrage of gunfire. Blue smoke from a dozen shots filled the air as the regiment, spurred into motion by the sound of mine own musket crack, attacked in kind.

Like a living shadow, the monster leapt away with the speed of a hellhound, nary a scratch upon its cursed form.

Darling, I beg of you—if you care anything for me—promise you will not leave the protection of the city walls, for I fear not just for your safety, but for your immortal soul. The Beast is truly evil incarnate.

In faith,

Gefrei

#

February the Twentieth

My brave Gefrei,

Each day I bend knee in the household chapel and pray for your swift return. I fear I am losing faith in the effectiveness of prayers, for we have heard nothing from you, and the countryside is rife with rumor. Papa says it's naught but gossip, but I'm beginning to feel I must see for myself that you are whole and hale. As unseemly as some might say, I believe myself a modern woman of action. I ride and shoot as well as any man. It suffocates me to busy my hands with pointless tasks like needlework, placidly awaiting news.

Impatiently,

Joe

#

February the Twenty-Third

My lovely Joséphine,

This is the last of my parchment and my heart aches that these letters have not yet been sent on to you. I could not fathom leaving them behind, so I salvaged the wrinkled pages from my saddlebags along with a few provisions after the horse went down. It pained me to put the wretched thing out of its misery, not just for the loss of a good mount, but for the waste of a musket ball. Supplies are limited.

Ereyesterday, as the sun went down, The Beast attacked the battalion. Once again, the foul brute moved with demonic speed and avoided injury. It darted amongst the horses, teeth and claws rending flesh. As a matter of decorum, I will avoid detailing the atrocities. I know you are not delicate, but even I shudder to recall the carnage. In the chaos, my mount took the bit between its teeth and bolted. I daresay it preserved my life.

For two days, The Beast has harried me into the foothills. I made for Langogne, but when the horse broke a leg in a rabbit hole, I knew there was no way I would make it afoot. I would rather pen these final words to you and warm my feet beside my campfire than make a futile, forced march down the mountain. It is here, upon the trail, that I shall make my stand.

Remember the day we met? When I saw you, dressed in men's breeches and hunting grouse in the wood, I was scandalized. And infinitely intrigued. At that moment, I envisioned you as my wife. I am no poet, but I pray these simple words convey the depth of my feelings for you.

The moon is rising, my love, and The Beast calls to it. Heed my words, stay off the mountain pass, for the demon cometh. It discriminates not between man and gentlewoman; it takes blood where it will. For me, I fear, there are only moments to sp~~

\#

February the Twenty-Fourth

Dearest Papa,

By the time you rise and read this, I shall be gone. I know better than to ask for your approval, and so while the household sleeps, I've stolen away. Please do not punish the stable boy, as I sent him on a false errand, then saddled my own mount.

It's been two turns of the moon since Gefrei left with the regiment to hunt The Beast of Gévaudan. In that time, there has been no word and I cannot remain, like a good mouse, waiting and wondering. That is not my nature, and I hope you love me for it, not despite it.

Try not to worry overmuch, Papa. I ride and shoot like a native huntsman, though I expect I'll only need use my rifle on the odd hare or partridge. The mountain path is quicker and less traveled than the river road and I expect to arrive in Langogne overmorrow or the day after. I'll send word when I'm able. All will be well.

Your devoted daughter,

Joe

The Tour Guide

"Welcome folks! My name is Debbi, and I'll be your guide today. Watch your step getting off the boat there, the edge is a little slippery. Hate to see you fall and break your neck. Again. Let's just gather over here. There's room for everyone if we squeeze in together. Don't worry—I won't bite unless you're into that kind of thing. Hahaha."

Ahem.

"What was that, Charon? Oh my. You, over there. The blonde in the back with the red sweatshirt. It seems you haven't paid the ferryman's fee. Two silvers, if you please."

What? That creepy, hooded guy didn't even say anything.

"Charon and I have worked together for quite some time now. We're totally in sync. Now if you just hand over the silvers, we have quite an agenda this morning. Time's a'wasting."

I don't seem to have any cash.

"Tut, tut. That's too bad. Everyone has to pay the ferryman. One way or another."

Ahhhhhhhhhh!

What was that?

Did you see that thing? It pulled him right into the river!

Oh, my God! Somebody help him!

"Ok folks, settle down, settle down. You should all just thank your lucky stars that *your* loved ones remembered to bury you with coin for the ferryman. No one gets a free ride. Now, if you will just follow me through this door, we have lots to see."

Man, it's warm in here.

"Delightful, isn't it? Of course, this is just a taste. The full effect is much more intense. Really scorching, with fire and brimstone and all that jazz. Well, if you're slated for that brand of torture. It really depends on your intake forms. But I'm getting ahead of myself. You'll all be sorted into the proper placements later. I'm just here to get you oriented and show you around a bit."

Excuse me?

"Yes, dearie?"

I...I think there's been some kind of mistake.

"Yes, yes. They all say that. Now if you just—"

No, I mean, I'm Buddhist.

"Why didn't you say so, love? You're definitely in the wrong place. If you just go with this nice fellow over here, he'll pop you over to the reincarnation office, right quick. Don't forget to ask for a refund for your ferry fee."

What the hell was that?

They just disappeared!

"Just a little demi-demon, nothing to worry your pretty little heads over. An errand boy, if you will. Definitely lower caste, but I do love the crackling noise they make when they teleport. Don't breathe in the smoke, though. I'm not entirely sure what it would do to you.

"Now, if you would just follow me. Watch your head there. You'd hate to poke your metaphysical eye out on your first day. There's plenty of time for that later. These stalagmites are kind of sharp. Or are they stalactites? I can never remember which point up and which hang down.

"Anyways, through this door over here are the classic Hell fires. Any Christians in the crowd? Speak up, don't be shy."

Me.

I guess I qualify. Non-practicing, but I was baptized.

Praise Jesus!

"Well, alright then. Simmer down, Jesus can't hear you. Besides, it's a little late for that, don'tcha think? Anywho. This is probably where you'll end up, if you were just a garden variety sinner. Liars. Thieves. You know, small potatoes. There's something a smidge more intimate for the darker souls. I won't ask you what you all did to land yourselves here. Not my job to judge.

"If you want to gather around the window to take a look, I think...oh yes! That hussy over there is about to fry. Crispy! Sorry, it's soundproof glass, so you won't get the full experience. The screams are really quite exquisite."

I think I'm going to be sick.

"Take a deep breath, sweetheart. It'll pass. Let's just move along down the hallway, why don't we? Single file around that puddle of acid, if you please. Hopefully, someone from maintenance will get that sorted soon. These leaks are getting worse and worse. There never seems to be enough money in the budget for repairs.

"But never mind. You don't care about all that red tape. We're just going to hang a left here...Ooops! Pardon us."

What the hell is that?

"That, my dears, is a Prince of Hell. What a real treat! This almost never happens outside of the second level. Let me introduce you to the great Prince Asmodeus. If any of you are here due to lustful misdeeds, you'll be spending quite a bit of time with this Beast."

Debbi, my dainty turtledove. Flattery will get you everywhere. Perhaps once you've offloaded this new troupe of damned souls, you might consider gracing me with your presence in my private quarters for a...drink?

"Asmodeus, please. I'm working."

Always the proper little succubi. So what do we have here? I sense a spirit amongst you that is craving the reaping. Yes, you with the raven locks. Do I detect the scent of rosewater shampoo?

Essential oils, Sir...M'lord...ummm?

Never fear, my pet. Before long, you will be begging to call me Master.

"Asmodeus, stop toying with the newbies. They haven't even registered yet."

As you wish, Debbi dearest. Don't forget—drinks at the witching hour. I promise, you will have no cause for regret.

"Don't you have souls to go torture? Off with you."

Adieu, for now, my dark goddess.

Wow. Is he for real?

What did he mean by the reaping? What's he going to do to me?

"Please, folks. Let's not speculate or get riled up. You never know where you'll end up until you've gone through the registration process. No need to put the cart before the horse. Not that the horses down here are the cart-pulling types. Nightmares, really. They breathe fire and induce screaming night terrors. Heart-pounding, spine tingly, awe inspiring, stupendous creatures.... Um, excuse me! You there! Stay with the group, please."

What's down there? I hear singing.

"Sorry, that area of the Afterlife is off limits. Non-sinners only. What you're hearing is Valhalla. The drinking and carousing is pretty fun, but after a while it feels a bit like a high school reunion. A bunch of over-the-hill jocks, I mean warriors, reliving past battles."

I see a white light!

"Yes, that's Elysium: sunshine, endless fields of golden grain...'No snow is there, nor heavy storm, nor ever rain'...How very dull. And don't even get me started on Heaven, down at the end there, with the manna and the clouds and the tedious harp music. Last year I had Gabriel in the office Christmas pool. Have you ever tried to shop for an Archangel? Such a tiresome prude!

"But I digress. Come now, if you focus your attention over here, I think you'll really enjoy this."

Ew, gross!

Yikes! Are those spiders?

That poor man.

Stop it! He's choking on them!

"Magnificent, isn't it? This is a personal hell, custom tailored to the victim's individual phobias. An impressive amount of creepy crawlies, isn't it? A lot of atheists end up in this sort of designer afterlife. It's more fitting, since they aren't ingrained with a lifetime of catechism-induced, fiery guilt."

Shit. That's going to be me.

"Language, darling. No need for vulgarities. As I said, no one knows for sure where they will be placed, but I'm sure the administration team will put you exactly where you need to be."

Oh, my God. I know that man. Mark? MARK!

"Please Miss, come away from the glass. He can't hear you. It's always unfortunate when you see someone you know during the tour. And let's not bring God into it. He's very busy.

"So sorry about the hoopla, everyone. I usually bring new sinners through the older sections to avoid this kind of drama—the back dungeons hold souls who've been here for centuries, unlikely to be friends of new arrivals. But they are hosting a mass flogging in Section Twelve today and that takes quite a bit of logistics to run smoothly. We would have been in the way. I hate to cause a ruckus for the administrative staff. They work so hard, the dears."

Oh, Mark...I didn't know...

"There, there, honey. Could someone please give her a hanky? Chivalry doesn't have to be dead, just because you are. Now, we really can't delay any longer. I have something really special to show you before I drop you off at registration."

Eeeeek!

"What? Oh, watch the snakes. Looks like we've had some escapees from one of the designer cells. Don't worry, they're keyed to a specific soul and won't bite."

Ow!

"Well, they won't unless you step on their tails. You had better sit down before the venom paralyzes you. Of course, it can't kill you, but this *is* Hell. It's going to sting a bit."

Mppphhh....owwwppphhh.

"Don't try to talk. I'll send someone to collect you once we get to registration.

"The rest of you, take a look over here. This is one of our special guests. He's been here for—well I'm not sure—long before my time. But it's my favorite customized punishment. I could watch for hours."

Is that Sisyphus?

"Right in one!"

I thought he was a myth!

Who's Sisyphus?

"Not much of a Greek scholar, are you? Not that I blame you, dreadfully droll stuff. The literature, not the actual people. They were quite audacious. Affairs with gods, epic adventures, battling mythical sea monsters in the flesh. Whew! Exciting times.

"The man you see here was once the king of Ephyra. I think you call it Corinth these days. It's hard to keep track of all the silly name changes you humans go through. I mean, why can't you pick a name for a place and stick with it?

"Anyways, a bit of an egomaniac, Sisyphus thought he was smarter than Zeus himself. Imagine! In punishment for his trickery and lies and ridiculous self-entitlement, he was condemned to roll a boulder up that hillside for all time. Wait for it...just before he gets to the top... Whhhhheeeeeeeee! Down it goes."

That's awful.

"Look, there he goes again, trudging along. Seems like hard work, doesn't it?"

Oh, man. Does he ever get it to the top?

"Nope! That's the genius of it. An eternity of almost, but never quite. Wheeeeeee! Sorry, it always gives me a giggle. Never gets old.

"Well, if you can tear away, I think we've just about come to the end of our tour. There's so much more to see, but there's never enough time to show it all. Don't be disappointed, you'll have lots of opportunities to experience it for yourselves. You are here for eternity, you know.

"If you come this way, I'll leave you here in registration. You can all take a seat until your name is called. Please grab a packet from the table as you go by. It's important to fill out the forms correctly. Three signatures on line seventeen B, but don't complete page twenty-three unless you answered yes to question one-hundred-seventy-four. Got it?"

Wait! There's over three hundred pages here.

"You're lucky. They've done away with the addendums R through W. You'll have about a decade to complete them, so there's plenty of time to take your time and do it right."

Ten years? We're just supposed to sit here listening to this crappy elevator music, filling out endless forms for ten years?

"In the scheme of things, that's not very long to wait, dearie. It's probably a mite nicer than where you're headed next."

These chairs are kind of uncomfortable.

I think my pen's run out of ink.

It's really stuffy in here.

I feel like I haven't slept for days. Is there any coffee?

"There's a pot in the corner. Help yourself."

It's empty.

"Well, let me remind you once again this *is* Hell. What were you expecting? Now, if there's nothing else, my shift is just about over and I have a date with a Demon Prince. A pleasure meeting you all. Good luck everyone and welcome to the Afterlife!"

Blind Weaving

The kind of web you weave depends on what you are hunting.

I string the border first, feeling my way from tree to tree. The circle must be strong, rope-thick, and cast wide enough to block the path. What good would it do me if my prey was able to wriggle beneath the trap?

Once the framework is finished, I add translucent runners like a starburst of glass filaments. They'll hold the pattern with its spirals and whirls. Unlike my smaller kin's webs—the recluses and orb spinners—prey will not fly mindlessly into this net. It must be drawn in.

It is important to choose the inner threads carefully. I make my color selections by touch. Bark rough browns. The silken greens of creeping vines. Here and there, a thorn-sharp crimson. The design must be precise and more than once, I tease the strands out and start again.

I cannot see the finished web, but I can tell when it is nearly right. My breath tickles the threads and the great woven eye shivers. It wants to blink. I add another length of the ropy vines along the top and give my masterpiece an eyelid. I sigh in contentment.

To create is to be divine.

Hunger gnaws in my belly. While the weaving soothes my impatience, I need to eat. To do so, I must wait. How I envy the sharp-eyed eagle, as she dives to snatch a mouse out of a sea of summer grass. Even the lame wolf is allowed to limp behind the pack and harry the rabbit. I cannot stalk my dinner by sight; I must rely on patience and trickery.

A single wire runs through the web, reaching high into the treetops. I scramble up the old oak trunk. The dryad inside sleeps, but even if she woke, she would not begrudge me a meal. We are old friends, she and I, both fond of our little deceptions. It is how old ones like us survive. I hook my many legs around her welcoming branches and settle in to wait for the wire to sing.

The day cools and the warmth of light on my back fades. It is better this way. If true dark falls, it will be too late, for the prey will go to its rest. However, in those liminal moments when the violet and gray twilight shadows grow, my target is brave. And foolish.

Footsteps crunch in the dried leaves. They pause and I can hear an intake of breath. A gust of wind ripples the canopy, and I hush it. *Be gone silly sprites, I am listening.* They caress my thorax, the cheeky vixens, before moving off and leaving me in peace.

I nudge the lead wire, and the eye blinks.

The prey squeaks and mumbles to itself. I try to understand the words—something about imagination and the wind? It is hard for me to remember what the sounds and syllables mean. I am sure I knew them once, but it has been centuries since I hatched beneath the bed in a mortal's humble cabin. One thing I do know, humans love to chatter meaninglessly. This one is too stupid to notice the wind sprites have gone, and the eye blinks on its own.

My quarry takes a step closer, graceless feet snapping small twigs. I imagine its face with wide eyes and a slack jaw. It smells nervous and amazed. I try not to preen. Of course, it should be awed. My work is meticulous. Have I not woven the pattern just so, to astonish and mystify?

The lead wire trembles. It is just a faint vibration as the human reaches out and gently touches the web. I ready myself to spring. Not yet. My trap is not sticky like the house spider's. It befuddles and disorients before it ensnares.

The vibration strengthens. I long to claim the sweet, tender flesh, but I must wait for sound and scent cues. I am at a disadvantage, and it rankles. Swinging my head back and forth, I listen for the rub of fabric and the whisper of breath.

There.

I can sense the prey's confusion as it explores my creation. A woven eye, strung across the path, where no eye should be. The scent of curiosity fills the air, as it leans closer to put both hands on the web. Touching. Exploring. Unafraid.

As I said, humans are stupid.

The eye blinks and the thick vines tangle about the prey's arms. It yelps and pulls back.

I lunge. The weave jangles and shimmies beneath me, but it knows me as creator, allowing me safe passage across the threads. Even in my ever-present darkness, my many feet are sure and swift, following the vibrations along the lines.

It takes but a moment to reach the center of the web and sink my fangs into my prey. I wish I could see its face, but I know that its terror is reflected in my eight blind eyes. My venom works quickly, and the struggle ends between sluggish heartbeats. I nibble and slurp until sated, then carefully dismantle the threads and re-wrap them around what is left of my dinner. Self-satisfied, I stroke the cocoon—its multi-colored strands make for a beautiful tapestry—rough and silken and prickly. I do love the artistry of it all.

The pinprick of tiny feet runs over my leg. A black widow crawls up to nestle in my carapace. It tickles, but I let her wriggle close.

Come now, little sister. Let us find you a safe place to lay your eggs. I will just hang my leftovers up in the oak tree for later. The dryad will not mind.

Flattened

Dark circles ringed Alice's eyes. Coffee cups and empty wine bottles littered her apartment as she exchanged one for the other, depending on the hour. Street maps and atlas pages covered every flat surface, scribbled annotations crammed in their margins. On each, the same area of the city center was circled and starred. Shaking fingers trailed over a satellite view of the highlighted block.

The damned road wasn't there. It was never there.

She let out a strangled shriek and swept the crinkled papers off the desk.

Slipping on her jacket, Alice floated down the stairs in a daze. She moved without thought, her feet compelled by phantom muscle-memory. Three lefts. Her heart rattled like popcorn on a hot stove. Two rights. Straight through the next intersection. She shifted foot to foot and stared down the mouth of a darkened side-street. A tattered paper map crushed in her clenched fist as she tried to control her breathing.

She'd arrived.

A mysterious, deserted thoroughfare had plagued Alice's dreams for months. The vivid images had felt real, but she couldn't find any record of the street in the municipal archives. After her third request to pour through the repository, the rumpled city clerk had shot her a worried look. He'd swallowed hard, pulled at his tie as if it strangled, then shoved a stack of photocopies at her and slammed the door in her face.

The stupid files had been no help. The street didn't appear in any of the archives. When she returned to city hall, the records clerk didn't answer the door. Tired of dealing with the crazy lady, she supposed. It didn't matter. The vision had shown the way—three lefts, two rights, straight through the next intersection.

And now here she was, peering down a street that didn't exist anywhere but in her dreams.

Alice glared down at the impossible-to-refold map in her hands. According to its insistent print, this dim avenue was a figment of her imagination. There was categorically, empirically, and historically no road between Swift Street and Poplar Lane. The bustling city agreed, its inhabitants busily ignoring this forgotten slice of antiquity as they went about their business.

One lane over from where she stood, neon signs cast rainbow-hued pools of light on the sidewalks. People hurried down the street, brushing elbows and peering into shop windows. Raucous laughter spilled from the crowded pubs and traffic hummed like a hive of overgrown bees.

In stark contrast, the boulevard in front of her was empty. Just like in her dream, asphalt transitioned to rough cobblestone and crowded storefronts gave way to sweeping, overgrown lawns. The night held invisible eyes, watching, biding their time.

An alarm flared in a blurry corner of Alice's mind. It was all too bizarre. She should go home and forget about this ill-advised adventure. Nothing good could come of exploring a shadow-drenched street no one else believed in.

She dismissed the thoughts as silly and over-cautious.

A gust of wind slipped icy fingers down her collar. It plucked at her lapels, an ethereal sprite tugging her forward. Gooseflesh dimpled her arms.

She shook herself, then stuffed the lying, traitorous map in an overflowing trash bin. The dream-vision twisted around her will and smokey, barely there tendrils drew her toward the unnamed street.

Alice squashed down the tiny, internal warning that begged her not to go. A louder voice marched around in her head—*find the tree.*

Glass crunched underfoot. The old-fashioned gas street lights, their lamps shattered, stood stiff-backed like skeletal sentinels. A crescent moon played hide-and-seek behind dilapidated houses. The ancient Victorians looked like gingerbread houses left to grow stale and moldy. Halfhearted moonlight struggled against the shadows, casting living braids of smoke and silver across the broken pavers. The odd tentacles reached for Alice, feathery kisses skating over her skin, beckoning her onward. She moved in a dreamlike haze, the way ahead both foreign and familiar.

The breeze returned to tousle her golden hair, like the fetid breath of some indiscernible beast on the back of her neck. It blew a sheet of wrinkled parchment down the road, a flattened, tattered tumbleweed. A second paper caught in the wind. For a moment it fluttered, pinned against a broken-toothed fence.

She looked closer. Not a tumbleweed, but a silhouette. The human-sized paper doll's printed mouth contorted in a silent howl. Alice shivered at the too-real details—a rumpled oxford, a loosened tie, a haunted look in its eyes. It reminded her of the disheveled clerk in the city records' office. She recalled the curious look he'd given her when she'd inquired about old lanes, missing from the street maps.

Her mouth went dry as she reached for the cutout. Her trembling finger grazed flat, dry cheeks. She snatched her hand back. It wasn't paper, but a leathery shell. A moment later, the wind snatched up the flattened silhouette and whipped it down the row with the fury of a miniature tempest.

Legs turned to jelly as Alice tumbled to the ground, face hidden in her hands. The weight of hidden apparitions pressed in on her. Ghostly claws pricked her, trying to pry her palms away. Unseen specters whispered in her ear, a thousand voices intertwining into an incomprehensible choir. Only one word stood out in the clarion:

Alice. Alice. AliceAlice. aaaalllliceAlicealicealicealice.

She struggled to her feet, powerless to resist the call.

A thousand steps led nowhere. The rough stonework beneath her feet blended together in an unchanging patchwork tapestry and the rows of crumbling houses became indistinguishable from one another. Time blurred, measured only by the rhythmic chanting of the eerie voices urging her onward.

Between one breath and the next, she arrived.

At the end of the never-ending road, a solitary tree grew like an expectant monolith. Mottled gray bark flecked its trunk with ashen scales, and gnarly roots wriggled snakelike from the ground, cracking the surrounding cobblestones with their blunt faces. Filament tongues tasted the air, searching, seeking.

Worms squirmed in Alice's stomach and icy sweat dotted her upper lip. This alone differed from the dream, and yet she knew, like a hummingbird drawn to the rose, that this was how the dream ended.

She blinked. An uncanny halo of light ringed the tree. Not the crisp, clean shine of starlight, but an oily glow that seemed to emanate from its wine-dark flowers. The blossoms glistened in the uncanny light—hundreds of questing mouths, drooling nectar like saliva. Branches dipped as if the monstrosity bowed in greeting.

Alice shrank back, but the wind whipped a coven of flat shapes around her, like a string of paper dolls blocking her retreat. Their lips never moved, but a rasped arcane ritual whispered in her ears.

Movement near her feet drew her gaze down. Her breath hitched as an inky serpent squirmed towards her, the black root wrapping around her legs. Tiny barbs sunk into her skin, striking with deadly fangs. Venom burned through her, and her vision swam.

Alice tried to wrench away, but a second tendril snaked around her wrist. She opened her mouth, and a whip of vine slithered down her throat. It gobbled up her scream. Lungs burned as the ropy creeper stole her air. Branches creaked, wrapping around her in a tender embrace. The flower mouths latched onto skin, sucking Alice dry. She sagged, but root and vine held her upright.

Petals smacked like lips, slurping, devouring. Finally sated, the flowers let out a chorus of contented sighs. The halo of light around the tree pulsed with renewed vitality. Overhead, the voices chattered, welcoming a newcomer to the symphony.

Out in the city, the neon bar lights flicked off and the late-night drinkers stumbled home. No one spared a glance for a blonde, flattened husk that scuttled in the breeze. The darkness deepened as the moon set on another voiceless tumbleweed, somersaulting down a street that only existed in dreams.

The Shadowman

When Momma left, she said, *stay away from the windows child, especially at night. Beware, lest the Shadowman is watching.*

But how would I know?

In the end, the solution was obvious. I propped Miss Izzy on the windowsill. My dollie was the perfect sentry—she needed no sleep and her button eyes never blinked. For days, she kept watch.

Movement in the yard!

I stiffened, feet rooted to the warped floorboards, until she gave the all clear. Not a goblin, but merely a fox, nosing in the woodpile, in search of a fat vole. I relaxed and made my way to the kitchen. There was enough food in the cupboards to keep me from going hungry while Momma made the journey to town. She'd trade the wild mushrooms and medicinal herbs we foraged in the forest's heart for essentials like salt and lamp oil.

I made myself a cheese sandwich, slicing the bread thin. Just in case.

When the dry goods ran out, I ventured into the root cellar and brought up jars of fruits and vegetables. "Are you hungry, Miss Izzy?"

You know I hate pickled beets.

I shrugged and fished them out of the jar, staining my lips red. Giggling, I looked at myself in the mirror—a smaller version of Momma, raven locks and a crimson smile. I pulled one of her many rainbow-colored, patchwork shawls from the closet and draped it over my shoulders. In my mind, I could hear her humming and I twirled in time to the familiar tune. My feet pounded in a syncopated rhythm.

Quiet now. The sun's about to set.

I shuddered. "Any sign of Momma?

Not yet.

Stomach churning, I folded the shawl into a neat square and put it away. I chalked another line on the slate. Twelve days. Momma had never been gone this long before. The nights grew darker as the moon waned, and the Shadowman gained strength.

Evening light shining through the window twisted like a kaleidoscope—liquid gold turning mauve and salmon, fading to velvet twilight. I lay on my pallet and cocooned myself in my blanket. As true night fell, the air chilled, slipping icy fingers down the chimney and pooling in the empty hearth. Soon I'd need to go out and bring in wood for a fire. It would have to wait until daylight.

It was known that this close to the dark moon, the Shadowman grew bolder. Even by day he lurked in shaded bowers, curled in the murky cracks in the stonewall. Fluid in form, he could hide within a hollowed tree, or squeeze beneath the porch steps. Always watching, biding his time.

I stared at the ceiling, willing sleep to come. Outside, the wind howled, a pack of translucent wolves scratching at the door. A narrow stripe of moonlight meandered across the floor. My breath caught in my throat. I imagined the Shadowman, poised behind that narrow silver ribbon, held back by the fragilest of barriers.

One more night. Rest now.

Leaving Izzy to her stalwart watch, I slumbered.

A silent figure stalked Momma on the wooded path. It loomed behind her, taller than Grandfather Oak, eyes burning like coals. Darker than void, even the forest's shadows trembled and drew back. The inky silhouette hulked like some amorphous beast.

I tried to shout—Behind you, Momma!—but the words froze in my throat. A claw reached out, plucking at her patchwork shawl.

Jerking upright, I woke to the rising sun. Sweat pasted my shift to my back and my throat felt raw, scraped by unleashed screams. I shuffled to the washbasin and splashed cool water on my face. My voice sounded froggy, as I asked Izzy the same question I had for days.

"Any sign of Momma?

My dollie stared at me for a moment, with her expressionless, black button eyes.

I think you'd best prepare. There'll be no moon tonight.

Acting bolder than I felt, I inched to the window and peered over the sill.

Dew glistened on the overgrown lawn, but none of the yard pixies sipped the fat drops. The sleek brown-striped adder that spent lazy mornings sunning atop the woodpile was nowhere to be seen. No birds warbled in the treetops. No small creatures rustled in the underbrush.

The forest held its breath.

In Momma's stillroom, I gathered up dried borage, horehound, and white willow bark. Herbs to protect against evil. I ground them to a fine powder and sprinkled them by the door and along the windowsills.

It won't be enough.

"I know!"

The only thing the Shadowman truly feared was the sun, but lantern light would keep him at bay. I poured the last of the oil, careful not to spill a precious drop. Balling my sweaty hands in my skirt, I prayed to the great goddess Cerridwen it would last the night.

Preparations finished, I nibbled on the rest of the beets. They left a lump in my stomach and a sweet and sour tang on my tongue as I waited for the sun to set.

Light faded, and I clutched flint and steel in my hands. My skin crawled, a voice in my head screaming to light the lamps. I hesitated. He would come at full dark. If I acted in haste, I would run out of oil too soon.

Outside, the diaphanous wolf pack sang in chorus, encouraging the sun to rest. Bit by bit, the glowing sphere slid behind the trees. Shadows lengthened. Miss Izzy scanned their depths, searching for his glowing eyes.

Light the lamps! Now!

I scurried forth, sparking the wicks. Warm pools of light filled the house.

The Shadowman laughed.

Douse the light, child, and let me in. The night is long, and I know you are alone.

His voice echoed in my head as he leaned on the doorframe. It creaked, but held, a strip of golden lamplight holding him back. I glared at the door, not daring to peer outside, and huddled in the light.

The wolf-wind quieted.

In the distance, a faint humming sounded. It drifted down the forest trail, coming closer.

"Momma?"

No! The Shadowman is a trickster.

The humming grew louder.

"Can you see her, Izzy?"

Stay back!

"Momma! Come to the light!" Drawn by her voice, I leaned out the window. "Quickly! The Shadowman has come!"

Footsteps pounded on the packed earth trail. A flicker of movement flashed between the trees. I urged her to run faster.

"The door, child!" Her voice came wild and breathless. "Let me in!"

In my haste, I knocked Izzy to the ground. The lamps flickered, oil nearly spent, as I flung open the door and searched wild-eyed for Momma.

The footsteps faded. Her voice mutated into wolf-wind song, then slowly faded away.

Silence draped the yard in a heavy mantle. Shadows quivered and bowed, bent like courtiers bowing to a tyrant king. The Shadowman swelled, taking their adulation as his due. His silhouette danced and twisted, as if the writhing darkness that made up his body could not decide on a shape. Horns curled from his head and brimstone eyes shone over a gaping maw.

He reached out a claw and dropped a bit of multi-hued fabric. Like a tame puppy, a gust of wolf-wind carried the tattered scrap across the yard. The translucent beastie nipped at my ankles as it dropped the familiar patches of Momma's shawl at my feet—shredded and stained a rusted red.

The Shadowman beckoned.

Come to me.

The lanterns died.

My mouth dropped open, but the scream that filled the night belonged to Izzy.

Nine Lives of Madness

It begins with a tickle. The Postman delivers a whispered prayer through the rift between dimensions.

Matron of Madness, hear my prayer...

I hear, but a single voice is not enough to draw me from my slumber. Rolling over in my nest of bones, I swat at the Postman with a sleepy tentacle. The creature snaps its beak at me and escapes through the rift.

It knows I cannot touch it.

I know it will return.

Such is the never-ending cycle of cosmic law.

#

The tickle becomes an itch as the Postman drops another invocation at my feet.

Eldritch Goddess, Slumbering Queen, show yourself...

They know not what they ask for. Please, just let me sleep.

The Postman fixes a beady eye on me. It bobs its head and spreads its wings, like some mortal crow pleased to deliver its unwanted gift.

I yawn, sharp-toothed maw wide, then click my jaws shut and pull my poppet close. It's gone all gray and floppy. Useless against the madness. I fling it aside, where soon it will be naught but more bones to line my nest.

The Postman shrieks and takes flight, excited for what's to come. While I still have clarity, I realize it too must be crazed. The thought feels familiar. How many times have I had this epiphany?

I lie back down, but sleep eludes me.

#

The Postman no longer stands by to watch my discomfort. Instead, the vile creature flings the petitions at me with no thought for the reverence in which they were offered and disappears through the growing rift to collect more.

Great Goddess, I implore you...

...I beseech you...

...I entreat you...

How many different words can humans use to say the same thing? Perhaps they have nuance, but my thoughts are fractured, battered by the voices. The prayers layer on top of one another, the requests becoming a jumbled roar in my ears.

...knowledge...

...vengeance...

...power...

#

My head aches. I tear at my face, claws ripping long gashes into my skin. Would that I could pluck the voices from my brain like wriggling maggots. They never cease their chatter, their cries of *grant me* and *deliver me.*

The wounds heal and I slash them open again. Ichor drips from my chin.

When the Postman returns, it carries no petitions in its sharp beak.

I am relieved. I am afraid.

Instead, a dark ribbon trails behind it, the end clutched in its talons.

As the ribbon winds around me, I can feel the human realm. A shadowed glade, full of cloaked figures. Flickering torches. A circle of salt and blood. Rhythmic chanting in an arcane tongue.

A voice rings out, loud against the backdrop of the others.

Once, every hundred generations, She may be summoned. Today we gather...

No, that seems wrong. Only a single generation. It's all the poppet can bear. Perhaps time flows differently here. My tentacles twitch, as the unknowing irritates like a spec of dirt in the eyes, a tiny thing that grates and burns. The idea of a poppet intrigues me though. A talisman to keep the voices at bay?

The thought is ripped away as the voice grows louder.

Koshna, Matron of Madness, Chaos incarnate, we summon you!

I howl and the heavens shake. For a moment I resist, but it is written in the stars. Even I cannot deny the call of my true name while awake. Why do they not just let me sleep?

I reach for the rift and crawl through.

The Postman cackles in delight.

#

My mouth tastes of copper and salt as my teeth rend flesh. The screams blend into a delicious harmony. No more petitions, no more prayers. Only a thousand voices wailing in wordless agony. I devour them all.

Above my head, the Postman soars, its broad wings blotting out the sun. The creature is no longer deliverer, but the herald of my destruction.

The brave stand against me, brandishing weapons that do nothing more than tickle. I open my arms and let the madness loose. Their minds melt as the tendrils of power touch them. They are not built to contain divine chaos.

A poppet is.

The thought stops me in my tracks. Becomes an obsession. I'm not sure what I'm looking for, but I race across the world.

This one. No. I tear its soul from its body.

That one. No. I use its jagged bones to pick my teeth.

Perhaps? Disappointment surges through me, as its mind turns to sludge.

There.

An oasis in the turmoil.

The creature is small, much smaller than the men that flee before me. I reach down to stroke its fur, and the insanity soaks into its tiny form.

It purrs.

I remember.

The voices still tear at me, but the poppet holds back the madness with a protective shield. Compassion. Empathy. It rubs its face against my legs.

I glance around at the destruction, the death I've brought to the world. This is my curse. If I could feel such things, I would know regret.

With my mind clear, I gather the poppet and return to the rift. As long as the talisman lives to ward off the madness, I can slumber. One generation among the stars, a hundred for mankind. A reprieve for us both.

My nest awaits.

#

My eyelids feel heavy, drooping closed as the poppet and I snuggle, preparing to sleep. Perhaps less a poppet, and more a living teddy bear. Its whiskers tickle my cheek.

Feathers ruffle and a petition drops in my lap, but all I hear is a comforting rumble in my ear. It occurs to me that Teddy has nine lives. Nine hundred generations in the human world. A luxurious nap.

Nothing can break the cycle, but for now, we sleep. In time, the humans will forget the chaos and destruction. They will summon me again. After Teddy soaks up nine lifetimes of madness.

The Postman settles in to wait.

Publication History

"Lemon Scented Bleach" 72 Hours of Insanity, Volume 5

"The Vigil" Wraith (Beyond Fantasy Series Book 6)

"Cake" Tales From the Moonlit Path: Demented Mother's Day Issue

"The Vast Enormity of the Sea" Through the Grinder, Darkly, TL;DR Press

"Inhale, Exhale" The Molotov Cocktail

"A Questionable Gift" Dream of Shadows

"Antique Photos" Writing Battle

"The Left Hand Twin" 72 Hour of Insanity, Volume 8

"Return to Sable Basin" Tales From the Moonlit Path: Bloody Valentine Issue

"Darla and the Clown" The Fourth Corona Book of Horror Stories

"Flattened" WayWords, Issue #4: Unreal

"Nine Lives of Madness" Curios, TL;DR Press

About the Author

MM Schreier is a classically trained vocalist who took up writing as therapy for a mid-life crisis.

Whether contemporary or speculative fiction, favorite stories are dark and rich in sensory details. Weird twists abound—fiction with just enough truth thrown in to make folks question. Or perhaps that's non-fiction that's somehow gotten twisted up in imagination.

A firm believer that people are not always exclusively right- or left-brained, in addition to creative pursuits, Schreier is on the Leadership Team for a robotics company and tutors maths and science to at-risk youth. After years of living in the Great White North, Schreier and a very spoiled Labrador Retriever have inched a bit south to become beach bums at Chilly by the Sea.

Read more at https://www.mmschreier.com.